For Sian, Dave and my Mother

(Article from the Ty Mawr Times)

Disappearance at Cerrig-Mor Head

It is almost a year now since local tradesman, David. P. Davies (Dai Chips) from the sleepy coastal village of Cerrig -Mor, disappeared without trace!

We returned to the small quiet hamlet to inquire of the police and locals about any further news. On our previous visit, the town seemed to be in shock at the loss of one of its inhabitants, the streets empty and windswept, a fierce gale blowing in from the West.

Dai was feared dead by locals and family alike, after he was last seen approaching the headland at around 11pm on the 3rd of February 2018. When police responded to a call from his fiancée after she found his note asking her for forgiveness, they spoke to the regulars at the Green Man, and then began a search, eventually finding his shoes and a wallet up on the Headland in the middle of the standing stones. They were wrapped in a plastic Co-op bag and held down with a house brick.

It is still the case that in 2019, no-one in the town has any ideas about his disappearance and many we spoke to reminded us that it has indeed been almost a year, "Didn't we have anything else to write about!" remonstrated a particularly annoyed local man. However, his friend Molly, a barperson from the Green Man thought that Dai was having money problems, she also said his personal life was in a difficult phase. Molly confided in our reporter that Dai Davies had told her on numerous occasions, that he wished to disappear and have an end to it all. After extensive searches involving locals, the Police and the Coastguard, the search was suspended and since then no further evidence has been found and with no body as proof, it seems that Dai

Davies is still to this day, missing presumed dead. We attempted to speak to his fiancée Delyth but she told us to go away because Dai Davies is, in her words "Dead but probably not buried."

This is still a live case so anyone with any further information can contact us in confidence and we will pass it on to the local constabulary.

List of Characters

Arwen – Our hero

Si – colleague and friend, a self-confessed geek, lives at home with his mother and father.

Dai – self-employed carpenter and Arwen`s estranged husband, he used to be the love of her life, missing presumed dead.

Delyth – Dai`s mistress and his live in lover until his presumed death in January 2018

Les from the Spar – Delyth`s ex

Rhiannon – Dai`s younger sister and Arwen`s best friend

Richard – Rhiannon`s husband

Owen – Arwen`s nephew

Uncle Albie – Dai`s widowed uncle

Barbara – Arwen's widowed Mother

Debbie – Arwen`s friend from Head Office

Glynys – cook at the centre, helps run the food bank and the Breakfast Club for the Elderly.

Pat Potatoes – gardener at the community centre community garden

Dai the Death – undertaker at Caradoc Jones and Jones

Agamemnon and Betty Upstairs – tenants in upstairs flat

Maggie Stamps – Café owner

Merlin and Gwendolin – Si`s best friends, founders of the Cerrig-Mor Magicians Community Group

Jude Jones – Sherlock`s Wife

Sherlock Jones – Private Investigator

Geoff Norman – Centre manager

Carys – Police Officer and Family Liaison Officer

Badger – Dai`s best friend and business partner

Lizzie – Cleaner at the centre

Albie`s carer Ken

Mam and Dad Davies – shadowy figures who live in North Wales waiting patiently for Rhiannon's ancient grandmother to shake off her mortal coils, so they can come home.

Stewart – Runs the poetry group

Alison – Runs the writing group

Arwen will be 45 years old in March 2019, She lives on her own in a terraced house that she and Dai (missing, presumed dead) bought when they got married and later converted into two flats when they realised they couldn`t have children. At the moment, Arwen lives in the bottom flat and an old lady and her large dog live upstairs. Arwen has a micro business making and selling inspirational bookmarks and works full time for the county council at the local community centre. She is an unpaid carer for Dai`s Uncle Albie and is still very bitter about her (presumed dead) husband running off to live with Delyth in her bungalow in May 2017. Arwen worries that this bitterness seeps through into her inspirational bookmark business. 2019 is the year she is going to change her life for the better.

Cerrig-Mor is a small faded but still beautiful seaside town, where everybody knows everybody. It is huddled into a small triangle with the sea on two sides and the Big House and farmland on the other. There is only one road into Cerrig-Mor, the sign bearing the town`s name is regularly adorned with slogans like "The town at the edge of the world" or "Abandon hope all ye who enter." The current one reads " The road to hell."

2019 was a year when Britain`s personality seemed to take a turn for the worse in many people's opinion. Still trying to leave the European union, and finally electing Boris Johnson as Prime Minister, to get the job done by the end of the year. Everyone was hoping that 2020 would bring better things, who would ever have guessed that an event was on the horizon that had us marooned in our homes and afraid to go near strangers as we scurried about our permitted business. So 2019 was the last year when we never thought about who we touched and took it as read that handwashing was something friends boasted about after they had been to the toilet and before they touched the peanuts on the bar.

25th December

2018

This journal is my Christmas present off Delyth so not surprised that it's preowned, she is very fond of the re-use and re-purpose concept, nothing wrong with that! But I am surprised and a little shocked that it was preowned by her boyfriend, or as I prefer to call him, my presumed-dead husband! I tried to work out if she knew he had written his bucket list and New Year resolutions in it and gave it to me anyway or whether she didn't bother to have a quick look through it before she wrapped it in last years crumpled Christmas paper featuring penguins in red scarves and festive bobble hats. The home-made tag read, "Have a Lovely Christmas Arwen, Love, Delyth, xxx."

To be fair, all she got off me (apart from my presumed-dead husband, which in my opinion was taking the re-use and re-purpose thing way too far!) was a bottle of Merlot that I found in the back of the cupboard, and a bookmark, and she only got those because Richard and Rhiannon invited her to the traditional family get together of mulled wine and nibbles on Christmas Eve. She should be lucky I am speaking to her at all, let alone giving her bottles of wine for Christmas after what she did to me. Delyth can thank Dai for that, if he hadn`t jumped off Cerrig-Mor Head, I would still be continuing my campaign of attrition towards her.

As she handed me the gift, she smiled at me, moved as if she was going to give me a cwtch and said, "Forgive and forget Arwen?" I assumed my hard face and was about to say something very rude when I noticed Rhiannon glaring at me over Delyth`s shoulder and repeatedly inclining her head towards Owen, so I just mumbled "I hate you Delyth" under my breath and delved into my carrier bag for the wine and a bespoke bookmark, featuring a bible scene and an edict from the ten commandments "do not commit adultery" in very ornate tiny script that is almost impossible to read.

Anyway, waste not want not as Greta Thunberg would say, it`s quite nice. This journal has a nice cover photo, a seascape which in my opinion looks a bit like

Cerrig-Mor. It`s practically unused apart from Dai`s New Year Resolutions and his bucket list. What is the difference between New Year Resolutions and a bucket list? I`ll look it up. Dai`s lists are ambitious to say the least, especially as he is missing, presumed-dead. Although he managed to do one, to be fair. The thing is though, when he wrote "Jumping off the Head for charity", I don`t think he meant jumping to his death as in suicide. The only charity that benefitted from his dive into the sea was the charity shop that Delyth donated his clothes to.

Dai`s New year resolutions 2018

Give up smoking

See more of family

Take up a new hobby

Win the lottery

Find a carer for Uncle Albie

<u>Dai`s bucket list 2018</u>

Climb Everest

Jump in the sea off the Head and for a charity

Go travelling

I like the idea of finding a carer for Uncle Albie, it`s a good one. I will get a well-earned break from the old bastard. I`ll talk to the family about that as soon as possible.

It`s still 2018 for a whole week, and what a bloody awful year it has been. Just as I was getting used to Dai living with Delyth and having to see them together in town, holding hands and wearing matching kagouls and trainers, he jumped off the headland into the sea after leaving a note saying he was sorry under a brick in the middle of the standing stones!

I can tell you if you think grieving for someone who has left you for a marriage wrecker is the same as grieving for a presumed dead person, you are very wrong, it is a whole new level of grief, even if you are not exactly in love with them anymore.

On top of that catastrophe, I got a new boss! Geoff Norman. I applied for his job but he had more qualifications and experience.

And then for the first year in the ten years since I have worked at the Cerrig-Mor community centre as Head Administrator, I didn't get my Christmas bonus! Why? I wrote this letter but haven't sent it yet.

Dear Mr ap-Gethin,

I wish to put in writing my dissatisfaction for not getting my Christmas Bonus. In spite of having worked for you for over 10 years. Perhaps this old tradition of a bonus has ceased since Geoff Norman has taken over as manager. Unless maybe, my contribution to the smooth running of the centre is no longer being taken into account. I feel quite depressed and sad and these feelings of neglect and of being undervalued are having a negative impact on my mental health.

Yours

That`s all I wrote, didn`t know how to end it, I thought yours faithfully was a bit lame, also it is a very whiney letter and doesn't fit in with my image of being strong and confident, so I am working to rule instead from now on, they will be sorry for their poor treatment of me! Do you have to tell your boss that you are working to rule?

Anyway, enough of the whinging! There are things to do before the year ends. I have to give the flat a good clean and a de-clutter and make a wall chart. I also want to sort out an Etsy page for bookmarks, online shopping is really taking off in Cerrig-Mor, I`ll ask Dianne for some help.

Off to bed now, on the settee as I want to watch the Miniaturist on the iPlayer and haven`t got anything to read because the charity shop book I bought last week has got some unidentifiable lumpy stains on page 10. Yeuch, my life is rubbish. Let`s hope 2019 is better.

I hope I can sleep better in 2019 as well! The thing is, I don`t believe Dai is dead, I need to get my head around it otherwise I`m going to wear myself out, trying to work out what really happened up on the Head.

2019

January

Look to the future

This journal *now* belongs to Arwen Davies, suck it up Dai!

Tuesday 1st January

1am

Just back from the New Year party at the community centre, it was not even ok, nearly everyone seemed to have a significant other except me, my life is awful, and worse of all, I can`t forget the Happy New Year kiss planted on my unsuspecting lips by Ciderman, who, as his name suggests is always stinking of cider. The sad part is that even *he* was with someone, his long suffering wife Sandra, who gave me a very nasty look as she batted the poor sod around the head and dragged him off.

3am

I can`t sleep. I still have six  more days off work. I am going to really organise everything this year, make lists etc and a chart to go on the wall, so I know every day what I am supposed to be doing. This is my list for 2019. I`m going to try and stick to it, although some will be hard to do, especially giving up smoking and being nicer, I am definitely not nice anymore, not on the inside anyway.

In 2019, I intend to

Give up smoking.

Go out more.

Find a new hobby.

Be nicer.

Be more interesting.

Do the lottery.

Find a new job.

Get a boyfriend.

Be a better daughter.

Be a better auntie.

Find a carer for Albie.

Write longer poems.

Find out what really happened to Dai.

N.B. Check list once a month to see if I'm on track. This is quite a long list but I have nothing to lose.

Wednesday 2nd January

11pm

Went around to check up on Uncle Albie before poetry group, took him some of the delicious turkey soup I had made, and Christmas cake. Uncle Albie thought the soup looked like sick, because the chopping blade had missed some of the carrots. I don`t know why he expects me to feed him every day, we have set him up with a home delivery service "Meals for You" which came highly recommended by Mam, but he still likes to have his tea cooked by me. I think he gets perverse enjoyment by criticising my cooking and comparing it to his ex-wife's Margaret`s efforts. She had the right idea, took her small son and buggered off decades ago, leaving Albie to his own devices. I keep threatening to do this, but only in my head.

At poetry group, I read out my very short poem,

Love was loud like fireworks,

Multicoloured, star bright,

Thinking of you always

Always,

Love, now all confused,

Infused with duty, fear, separation, and despair,

Damp with tears, drowned in recrimination,

*The stars shut out by dark clouds and dangerous
fog bound thinking.*

Then had to listen to Leonard reading his very long poem about how the mountains looked down on the sea, in winter, in the rain. I really like Stewart but he is rubbish at controlling the poetry group poets, all he does is sit there and occasionally says "Now, now!" when the arguments look as if they might get physical.

Made a chart to go on the wall, it's really boring. I need to get out more this year. To be fair, I get invited out a lot, but I am too grumpy and they soon regret their invitation. Does visiting family count as going out?

I thought I might add in other things that I do as I remember them, like Co-op, recycling. Writing in rubbish days would be good because I keep forgetting to put it out it now that it's moved to once a fortnight, I had better make another chart over a fortnight instead of a week, although if I made a monthly chart, I could put my pay day in as well. Great, I will get onto that tomorrow.

Thursday 3rd January

7pm

While I was standing in the kitchen waiting for my mushroom tagliatelle to cook, I studied my weekly chart which I have sellotaped to the fridge freezer. It`s pathetic, next year I will be middle aged, (45 years old) probably perimenopausal according to Dianne, I have only had one boyfriend who I then married, who then left me for a woman who can cook, and the highlights of my life are.

1. Going to Mam`s every Friday with fish and chips.
2. Going to Rhiannon`s every Sunday for lunch.
3. Going to poetry group once a month.

Maybe it`s because it`s January and it`s cold and dark and there are no prospects of anything getting better. I have to change things this year; my life is incredibly fucking boring! If I died now, nobody would even find me until tomorrow night because I would have failed to turn up at Mam`s with the chips. On my headstone, all it would say was,

"She was alive, but not very good at it, then she died"

11pm

The monthly chart doesn't work really. Apart from the fact that it only serves to highlight how little I do, I realise that putting down events on a 4-weekly rota doesn't take into account the calendar month difference or future events. I would be better off with a wall calendar chart thing, going to get one tomorrow from the "Just a Pound" shop.

Tomorrow I am definitely going for a walk down the beach. If I had bought my wall calendar today, I could have written going for a walk on beach on it, never mind.

I've got an appointment with "Hair for U" at 2pm on Saturday, I deserve a bit of pampering and a nice haircut.

Friday 4th January

11pm

I went out early this morning and bought the wall chart thing, it's huge! I love the "Just a Pound" shop. When it first opened, everyone said they were not going to shop there, including me, but after a couple of days, I went in just for a look, turns out, so had everyone else, now I meet people I know all the time in there, selecting cut price shampoo or deciding which plastic butterfly windmill to buy, they say, "Hiya, look at this, only a pound, fantastic!" and I agree with them, what did we do before we had a pound shop? I can`t remember.

Bought some football patterned wrapping paper and a birthday card for Owen, so hard to choose isn't it, got an auntie one in the end. It has a skateboard on it and says what a fantastic nephew he is in big blue letters.

I hung up the wall chart in the kitchen. I will fill it in tomorrow. I was going to go for a walk on the way back from Mam`s, but by the time I checked up on Albie and gave him his tea it was dark and raining, I`ll definitely go tomorrow. Looked for a new job on Indeed, didn`t find one. If I could find one I could resign from my job at the centre, then they would realise that giving the manager`s job to Geoff Norman instead of me, was the biggest mistake they have ever made.

Have written, going for a walk down beach on wall chart, sorted

---

HAIR FOR U!

*Perms a Speciality!

*Qualified Stylists and Colourists

*Complementary Tea & Coffee

Est 1990

Saturday 5th January

Saturday 5th January

11pm

I went to the hairdressers. Thank God for bobble hats and thank God it is so cold that I stuffed one into my bag before I left the flat. That bastard Carrie from Hair for U scalped me, the bastard! I have tried to measure what`s left, it`s about 1.5 inches long. And that`s stretching it!

Distracted myself from thinking about my lack of hair by sorting through my CDs. Successfully distracted myself so well that when I went into the bathroom, I nearly died of shock when I looked in the mirror over the sink!

Sunday 6th January

Wrap Owen's birthday football

Meet others at the pub

11pm

Picked up Mam and Uncle Albie. Sunday lunch at pub for Owen's 14th Birthday. Lovely! Because I am trying to be a better Auntie, I sat next to him and laughed at all the jokes from the joke book my mother got him, even the ones I didn't get. Most of us had burgers but I had pork chops. Mam kept on about how rude it was to wear a hat at the table, so I took my bobble hat off, that shut her up! Back to Rhiannon's afterwards for birthday cake and a game of football!

While I was in the pub, I unobtrusively checked out the men of my age, searching for a potential boyfriend as I am determined to get one this year. Sorry, they have no chance, I don't know what I was thinking of, rather be on my own. Perhaps I should cross "Find a boyfriend" off my list. I could get a lodger instead.

This wall calendar thing isn't working, it's so complicated, I stood in the kitchen this morning looking at all those garish multicoloured rectangles. It gave me a headache! I'm going to stick with the ad-hoc lists instead, I can write them in this journal.

I absolutely love my family. Except Uncle Albie who I have to care for but who is a horrible old man and not even my real uncle! I blame Dai, for jumping off the headland (if he actually did) taking my sense of fucking duty for granted.

Rhiannon and I are always fantasising about putting Albie in an old people's home, but we can't bring ourselves to talk to him about it. Definitely need to get him a carer, especially now that he has sacked his cleaner and is threatening to end his "Meals for You" contract because the food is rubbish, I can't disagree with him there, although Mam, who used to be a domestic science teacher and is a really good cook, seems to think they are ok. It's bad enough having to cope with the cleaning and supplementing his diet with my teatime offerings, let alone having to supply meals for the whole day.

Mam can also be quite difficult to love, but she is my mother, so I cut her quite a lot of slack, although she would say that she cuts me quite a lot of slack as well! At least she cleans her own toilet and doesn't pretend the washing machine instructions are beyond her. For the time being anyway.

Monday 7th January

11pm

Back to work this morning, still quietly seething with resentment about the Christmas bonus, finished exactly on time, then went to Uncle Albie's flat to tackle his dirty washing and warm up his half of the tinned chicken pie, that I bought for a pound. Work again by 7pm for an emergency meeting of the local "Dogs are not just for Christmas" committee, apparently the treasurer has resigned and popped off to Spain for a bit with the money, then home by 9pm. Caught up on Victoria Derbyshire, The Daily Politics and Newsnight. Trump playing up again, PM May's reshuffle was boring, I was looking forward to that, bought another book from the charity shop, checked the pages for cleanliness first, so can go to bed tonight. Horrible out there, so didn`t go for a walk, will go tomorrow.

I used to love my job; think I hate it now. Bastard Geoff, I bet he got his Christmas bonus. I will never offer to do them any favours ever again. All the bastard times I turned up on short notice when someone was off sick just to help out at the "Small Minds" after school club, putting up with the fighting and the sick and the tasteless ham sandwiches, and this is how they repay me.

Tuesday 8th January

11pm

Si is still on leave so I had to work today (On my day off Geoff Norman!)

Accidentally sorted out the problem with my National Insurance Contributions, I spent ages on the phone trying to get through to HMRC to rant about the demand for payment before I realised it wasn`t actually an income tax demand. Luckily, they kept me on hold for so long that I read the letter again, properly. They didn`t want more money at all, they were just giving me information about my pension. Apparently I am going to be working until I die of old age.

I was reading the free paper during my break this afternoon, when I came across an article on missing persons, from what I can remember, about 5,000 people of the 170,000 people who go missing every year, will still be missing a year later. Not all of these will be dead, a lot of them have just decided to run away to a new, hopefully better life.

Popped into Albie`s, made him some beans and eggs on toast. Unfortunately, today`s "Meals for You" was Spaghetti Carbonara and he hates that, he said he was starving so I gave him my packet of gingernut biscuits to cheer him up, it must be crap getting to his age and not having any friends to moan at or about. He snatched the biscuits, ripped the packet open and said "Ta" before dunking one in his tea and shoving the whole thing into his mouth!

Phoned Mam because I am trying to be a better daughter, to check that she had food to eat instead of the carbonara from "Meals for You" (not her favourite either) but luckily she has just topped up her freezer with a supply of supermarket ready meals and leftover home-made beef stew (She refers to beef and carrot stew as her "signature dish", been watching too many posh cookery programmes I think) she gave the carbonara to next door`s dog.

Wednesday 9th January

11pm

Si was back in work today, sporting a new grey sweatshirt with "Scouting for trolls" emblazoned on the front in gothic text. Never one for small talk, he got straight down to business.

"Wow! You`ve been scalped! Who did that?"

"Carrie from Hair for U" I said, "Apparently, she thinks I`m the girl you dumped her for, in spite of the huge age and IQ difference and my hatred of graphic novels and beards" To be fair, he looked mortified, I said "I don`t want to talk about it Si."

"Suits you mind" he said "Did you know that human hair grows at the rate of…"

"Stop right there" I said scowling, "Of course I know." I didn`t know, googled it when he went to the toilet. According to google, hair grows about ½ an inch every month.

Went to clean Uncle Albie's flat after work, it took ages, I'm exhausted, I don't know what he does with that toilet, rents it out to a troop of boy scouts maybe. I have no idea how caring for Albie became my responsibility, but I'm stuck with it for now.

Decided to sleep on the sofa and watch Prime Ministers questions and Victoria Derbyshire on the iPlayer. Loads of trouble brewing with the NHS crisis but it's all cwtchy here on the sofa with the tv to keep me company, so why should I care! Perhaps I should sleep on the sofa permanently or move the tv into the bedroom?

Friday 11th January

11pm

Had an extended lunchtime meeting with Dianne from head office. It was supposed to be a meeting about a new monthly magazine the head office was trialling and she gave me a list of stuff I had to email her every month. But we moved on eventually to my problems about new ideas to kick start inspirational bookmarks online and restart teaching meditation, but first, a long scary moan about how she is finally through the perimenopause and into the full-on menopause now. We sat outside because of the hot flushes and bought coffee from the kiosk; the tide was in, so lovely big waves. We had to keep moving our chairs so we could stay in the sun. The only problem with having a meeting on the seafront on a sunny day was she kept seeing people we knew and inviting them over for a chat and a catch-up, her and Mam probably know everyone in town between them and can name most of their kids as well. As we were finishing up Dianne asked how working with Geoff Norman was going, so the conversation degenerated into a quick moan-fest about my boss and her boss, Wynford ap Gethin, at head office, I`m beginning to think that Geoff isn't so bad really, at least his office is upstairs, Wynford sits facing her across a vast oak desk, upon which no amount of paperwork could be stacked high enough to evade his glares and inquisitiveness.

Ideas

If I make one bookmark every day, I will have over three hundred by the time the big Christmas fair comes around. Yay!

*Etsy shop

*Restart Meditation group (probably not in the right mind set for this, to be honest, the last one I did ended with me confiding to the poor sods who attended, that I hate people really. I`ll never forget the startled looks on their face as they filed past me on the way out, and when I saw one of them in town, I swear she ran into the Spar just to avoid talking to me.)

*Turning upstairs flat into a holiday flat when Betty Upstairs moves or dies (Betty is a lot older than me and smokes like a trooper!)

Called into Albie`s after Mam`s, big problem up there, some one seems to have moved in, he said he is a long-lost friend, phoned Rhiannon to ask for her advice, she sent Richard down to see what he thinks. He thinks it`s ok, this Ken seems a decent bloke and that because Albie has capacity, he is entitled to have a friend to stay, so we will just have to keep an eye on things. Had a quick look at Etsy, will set up page soon. Been a really busy week, a bit worried that my boss has seen my change of attitude re lack of bonus, c`est la vie, if he has, it`s tough. Going to watch Daily politics on the iPlayer.

Hooray! It`s the weekend! First craft fair of the year tomorrow! Yay!

We're Back!

Weeble's Craft Fair 2019 at the Community Centre

Every Saturday from (12/01/2019) 10 – 4

Come along and grab a bargain!

Loads of stalls : *Fresh veg, Bric a Brac, Crafts*

Refreshments available

Coffee and a Chat Café also open (10-3 Next to the fresh produce table)

<u>NB: PLEASE USE THE UMBRELLA STAND BY</u>
<u>THE GARDEN DOORS WHEN IT`S RAINING</u>
<u>OTHERWISE THERE ARE PUDDLES</u>
<u>EVERYWHERE</u>

Saturday 12th January

11pm

Some journal keepers give their journal a name apparently, so I`m going to give it a go, I've decided to call my journal Mrs Mayberry.

Dear Mrs Mayberry,

the first craft fair of the year was really quiet, everyone kept coming over to my table and saying "Quiet innit." Went to Uncle Albie's after craft fair to check up on him. His visitor is still there, camped out on the living room floor on the spare mattress. Signs of him having taken over Uncle Albie`s flat are everywhere! I say to Uncle Albie, do you want him to stay here, this friend, he says he has been asking him to leave, because he is fed up with him now. Right, I said, I will sort it out.

I squared up to Ken and said, "You have to go now, right now, pack up your stuff immediately!" After an hour of him arguing very politely with me that Albie was actually fine with him staying, just having a hissy fit because Ken asked him to help with the dishwashing, Ken left. Unbelievable. He was trying to bribe Uncle Albie into letting him stay by offering to take him to the pub for dinner, so in the end I had to take Uncle Albie out instead! Good thing is though, this bloke obviously has a sorting out and cleaning problem, because Uncle Albie`s flat is spotless! He even cleaned the toilet properly! So, nothing for me to do there today, he had even taken the recycling out! I felt a bit bad accusing him of taking advantage of Uncle Albie, using his washing machine to wash his clothes with and all the time trying to ignore the fact that he had washed Uncle Albie's clothes as well, had ironed them and had them folded neatly on the radiators. He tried to make out that Uncle Albie had put a few things in the machine for him as a favour, I just laughed, "Right, you are telling me that Uncle Albie did it are you?" He looked a bit guilty then and looked to Albie for confirmation but Uncle was shuffling off as quickly as he could manage, to the toilet.

Ken had made a space for his laptop by moving the settee and had his various shoes lined up alongside Uncle Albie's in the hallway. But to be fair, the kitchen was bleached to perfection, he had even bleached the washing up bowl. I waited patiently while he packed all his belongings into a large rucksack, then Albie and I followed him out of the flat and went to the pub. Afterwards I dropped Albie home, went to the Co-op, and bought my usual vegetable contribution of broccoli and carrots for Sunday lunch tomorrow. Having a really lazy night again, watching Poldark. Had a quick look on Indeed for jobs, there is a vacancy in the Chemist`s shop for a counter assistant, if it is still there tomorrow, I am going to apply for it.

Sunday 13th January

11pm

Decided that giving your journal a fucking name is stupid!

Went to Rhiannon's for Sunday lunch. Mam had been having a moan on Owen`s birthday about eating a lonely

Sunday lunch while we all got together, so Richard decided that from now on she is joining the rest of us every Sunday, I offered to pick her up but he said he was going to do it and I could just carry on giving Albie a lift, if that was ok. She glared at me and said, "How kind Richard is" and to be fair I feel really guilty about leaving her on her own every Sunday, I felt like such a fucking bad daughter. When I mentioned this to Rhiannon, she reminded me that Dai and I used to alternate our Sundays, one with my Mam and the next at her and Richard`s until Mam told me in January 2015 that she was fed up with cooking on Sundays and one of her new year resolutions was to use Sunday for God related activities in the morning and catching up on Coronation street and Emmerdale in the afternoon. I`d forgotten about that, and this is why Rhiannon is my best friend as well as my brilliant sister-in-law! Nice really, all of us being together. Uncle Albie was a bit funny, couldn`t wait to get home, so I knew something was up. I said that I was coming to his flat to check up on the washing powder, but he wouldn`t let me, then I realised that he had probably let that homeless man back in, so waited a couple of minutes then used my key to let myself in.

Idiot, he said it was my fault because I forgot to shut the door properly yesterday. Anyway, this Ken had turned up again and offered him £200 in arrears, to stay for a couple of weeks so Uncle Albie agreed, I am so annoyed about it but there again, if he cleans the flat it could be like a holiday for me. Every cloud, eh?

Monday 14th January

Start the one bookmark a day thing

Halfway through the month, my life is still boring, in the future, when someone finds this journal, they would probably given up reading it by now, fucking so boring.

11pm

Intern had taken over my desk and computer with the blessings of Geoff, he is supposed to be shadowing the centre manager not sitting in reception chatting to Si about War Hammer! So I noisily seethed away while doing things like cleaning the IT suite and sorting out the cutlery drawer in the kitchen. I refused Geoff's offer to run and get us all a Greggs cappuccino, so he knows I am annoyed about something. Called in Uncle Albies on way home, told the new lodger that he was a right bastard, taking advantage of a vulnerable person. He tried to sweet talk me, but I just ignored him, couldn't help noticing how clean the toilet bowl is, I think he has ocd or something, either that or he is trying to impress Uncle Albie and make himself indispensable. I shout back to him that I hope he didn't think that cleaning the flat and cooking dinner was going to substitute for paying the rent, because if he did, he had better pack his bag again.

Arghhh! Between the homeless man and the computer stealing intern I have had enough today. Applied for the job in the chemists, online.

It was such a relief not having to clean Uncle Albie's toilet, if I'm being perfectly honest, I am torn between his so-called lodger taking advantage of him and being relieved that someone is looking after him for now.

Maybe I could check out his background and do a deal with him, he could clear out the back bedroom at Uncle Albie's flat and stay there as a live-in carer while me and Rhiannon decide what to do with the old bastard. I could just pop in every day to make sure it's working out. No more cooking, cleaning etc, I`ll phone Rhiannon tomorrow, to see what she thinks. I`m sure she will agree that`s it a good idea.

Tuesday 15th January

Clear the desk to start the bookmark thing

11pm

Geoff was away this morning, doing something with his family, so I had to work on my day off! The Big Boss from head office unexpectedly called in. I requested a private meeting with him in the Tom Jones Sanctuary room and told him that I thought we should all have received our Christmas bonus by now. He was sorry I was upset and said he would bring it up with Geoff. Then Geoff got back and I had to have a meeting with him, he was a bit shocked that I was so angry about it, asked me if that`s why I have been in a really bad mood lately, I put my perplexed face on and said "Me! Bad mood? Nah, oops, got to run, time to set up for Italian Coffee and Conversations!"

Phew. Bonus will go in with our next pay day, I hope they all are grateful for this, told Si and he hadn't even noticed the lack of bonus. Anyway, I've stopped working to rule now.

Uncle Albie didn't want me to sort out his tea today because Ken has made spaghetti bolognaise. I have told Ken that I'll pop around soon with Rhiannon to talk about how he could stay and become Alfie's live-in carer. He seemed really pleased with that, especially as I also apologised at the same time for all the shit things I said about him.

Thursday 17th January

Get a big box for clearing the desk

Meeting at Albies

Try not to be boring

11pm

Me and Rhiannon went to Uncle Albies's flat for the meeting with him and Ken, I was a bit nervous because I thought he may have scarpered and my plans for a better life would come to nothing, Rhiannon was nervous in case we were giving a mass murderer access to an elderly man, but, as I pointed out, he has been there a while now, and Albie is still very much alive and obnoxious.

We sat at the dining table, Rhiannon had a notebook, and a very official looking form. I had a load of questions to ask like what's your full name and date of birth and have you been in prison and do you have any family and where are you from.

The answers were –

Kenneth O`Keefe 1/1/ 1964

No,

No,

Bodmin.

Apparently, he met Uncle Albie in the Spar when Albie went there to buy his tobacco and withdraw his pension. Ken thought Albie was someone he knew so they got talking, and they got on so well, that Albie invited him back for lunch. A likely story! Albie gave me a very sheepish grin as Ken told us this.

We agreed that Ken, can apply for carer`s allowance and can live at Albies rent free with Sundays and possibly Saturdays off. We are going to cancel "Meals for You" because Ken is going to cook. I am going to pop in every Wednesday for a catch-up and will still pick Albie up as usual on Sunday for lunch at Rhiannon's. Richard is going to get Ken checked out as a suitable person as soon as possible, I didn't know Richard could do that, but when I said so, Rhiannon kicked me under the table, so I shut up. After I had said "OWWW!" that is.

"Of course he can" she said, "that's his job Arwen!" She passed the form she had brought with her over to Ken and asked him to fill it in and give it to me next Wednesday.

As I walked Rhiannon back to her car, she explained that it was a lie about Richard being able to check up on Ken, but it will do until we find out how to do it for real. I didn't mention that Bodmin is famous for the jail, I thought that might complicate things. Woohoo! Can now cross "Find Albie a carer" off my list.

Dai and I would have been married 21 years today (January 17th 1998) brass is the traditional gift for your 21st anniversary. I quite like brass, turns up a lot in charity shops, in fact I have a tray shaped like a fish sitting on the table by the front door, I paid £2 for it from the "Pets Need Homes" charity shop in town. I keep keys in it. When Dai left, he threw his set of keys into it, they are still there, I can still hear the sound they made as they landed in the tray.

Friday 18th January

Ask mam if I can look in garage for a box

Be less boring

11pm

Took fish and chips up to Mam`s, she had kept her rhubarb crumble and custard from lunchtime, so we had that for afters. I asked her if I could look for a box but she said no, she needed all her boxes because she had started on her "Death Cleaning"! Apparently this is all the rage now for older people, she has a book and gave it to me for a borrow until next Friday. Before she handed it over, she wrote her name and phone number on the inside, I said "For God`s sake Mam!" she replied," I know what you are like Arwen, always losing things." I once lost my new geometry set in 1980 something, she was furious and ever since I have been given this reputation for losing things.

Anyway, this book from Amazon was a serendipitous mistake, because when she was buying it her reading glasses were in the bedroom and she couldn`t be bothered to get up off the settee to go and fetch them. She thought it said, "Change your life with Depth Cleaning" and had bought it for Cyril next door whose kitchen is disgusting. When it arrived, she was shocked to see it was "Change your life with Death Cleaning." It took her two days to look inside it, she is very afraid of the D word since she reached eighty.

I said, "Can I have a box to carry the book in? I`ll have a quick look in the garage, is it?"

She fussed about and said "No! stop nagging Arwen and grow up!"

I love winding her up, had a quick look at the book later, it`s mostly about decluttering your home on an epic scale, as if you are planning to die next week or something.

Sat 19th January

Craft fair

Find a box

11pm

It was very quiet at the craft fair again, Si came and sat at my table for a bit and listened to me moaning on and on about Delyth and Dai and how I should have been celebrating my wedding anniversary. I can`t believe Dai is dead, in the same way I couldn`t believe he buggered of with Delyth, citing a large bright green (whole) caterpillar in his home-made cauliflower cheese as the last straw.

The thing is, I don't believe he *is* dead. He is not the type to throw himself into the sea, he would have taken one look at the jagged rocks and changed his mind, and when my father died, I knew he was dead. Dai just doesn't *feel* dead to me and I`m going to find a way to prove that he is alive and kicking somewhere. I`ll have to bite the bullet and make friends with Delyth. I`ll call her tomorrow and arrange to meet her in Luigi`s to go over her last days with Dai.

Sunday 20th January

Phone Delyth

Find a fucking box!

11pm

Went to Rhiannon's for dinner, played scrabble afterwards, it really cheered everyone up, Rhiannon suggested to Owen yesterday that he should invite his best friends Alice and Charlie around after lunch today, so we were a very loud large noisy lot. When Charlie`s dad came to pick him up later, he spent ages at the door with Richard reminiscing about Sundays around the kitchen table playing board games, so he is invited now as well.

When he told Rhiannon she uncharacteristically told Richard off for this, he just said that Derrick was lonely since his wife left, as he said this, he sort of winked and inclined his head towards me! Rhiannon's eyes popped practically out of her head and she said in a very mean voice, "I`ll speak to you later Mister!"

I said, "I can find my own middle aged lonely men, thank you very much Richard" I gave him a nudge and added "Love you for thinking of me though, you big idiot!"

Phoned Delyth, I hate her, Meeting for coffee tomorrow.

Discovered the difference between a diary and a journal. Phew!! This is good because my life is so boring its`s hard to write anything down sometimes, so only interesting stuff from now on thank God!

A journal is

Personal written record of thoughts and experiences

Doesn`t have to be daily (!!!!! Yay!)

Honesty with yourself

Useful for venting toxic thoughts and bottled-up emotions

Like talking to a friend

Secret thoughts stay secret forever

I'm not going to lie in this journal or sugarcoat things. It`s going to be the unadulterated truth. Unlike my diary entry for the sixteenth of August 1999 where I wrote "Had a lovely day at the beach," when in fact it should have read, "Day at the beach started well, then Dai got very drunk on cider and puked over a crab."

Ye Old Oak is advertising for bar staff, could tick at least three boxes with this job, social opportunities, more money, and might meet a potential boyfriend!

Monday 21st January

Meet Delyth at 4.30

Find a box

11pm

Met Delyth at Luigi`s for coffee after work. I know I shouldn`t say this, but Delyth is really thick. I, on the other hand have a BA (hons) in Social Science and History so she thinks I`m really clever and is slightly in awe of me because of the science bit. She starts a lot of conversations with "With you being a scientist Arwen … blah blah." I have tried to explain it to her, but I've given up and who knows, maybe she is right and I should claim the label of scientist! Anyway, I went early to Luigi's armed with a pound shop notebook, five sections, just in case Delyth was deluded enough to think this was my hand reaching out in friendship. That ship had sailed when she stole my husband and was hurled into an everlasting storm when she came up with platitudes to justify her robbery, such as

"There's no smoke without fire"

"It takes two to tango"

"If it wasn't me, it would be someone else"

When I told Mam the things she had said, Mam replied "Well, she's not wrong." Unbelievable! Anyway, I tried to put those hurtful words out of my mind as I laid the notebook out in front of me and arranged my biros. I had already written the questions, one for each section, this was going to be an ongoing investigation.

1 Do you think he's dead?

2 What was his last day with you like?

3 What was he wearing?

4 Did he take anything with him? *Grandad used to bugger off when he'd had enough, and Grandma would only know when she got around to checking the bathroom for his toothbrush. I remember once when I was in junior school and our homework was "Ask*

someone from the older generation for advice," and his was *"Always take your toothbrush."*

5 Any other information that might be relevant?

Delyth waltzed into the café, long sun bleached hair tied up in a hippy scarf, making me look like a grumpy gnome in my red bobble hat. "Oh Arwen" she bleated as she rushed towards me, I held my notebook up, as if it were a shield, and said "Stop! We are here to discuss Dai`s disappearance, this is not a bloody social catch-up!" her face fell, so I added with a smile, "Sorry, bad hair day" Her eyes flickered to my bobble hat, but she said nothing, it must have cost her a lot not to say anything, so I went and bought her a cappuccino.

Answers

Do you think he`s dead?

"Well, we know he is dead Arwen, we found the shoes and then he sent those letters," Delyth pulls out a battered note from her slouchy hippy bag and flattens it out in front of her. "He has been gone for nearly a year now, and no word, not a flicker of hope from the police, I am trying desperately to move on. Trying to distract myself, joining clubs, dancing, karaoke, volunteering, looking for a little job"

It`s starting to sound like my good intentions list, so I butted in and pointed out that his body had not turned up, she said, "Yes, but as a scientist Arwen, you must know what happens to bodies in the sea."

"Everyone knows that Delyth, not just scientists, so apart from that, what other proof is there that he's dead?"

"Why Arwen, would he put me through this if he was out there, living his best life!" "And what about this!" she shoves the crumpled letter across the table at me. It was written on that posh cream paper with their address pre-printed at the top. I had to make do with bog standard A4 copier paper.

Delyth and David Davies

20 The Pines

Cerrig-Mor

My Darling Delyth,

can't handle it anymore, <u>YOU</u> have done nothing wrong, you are better off without me, be kind to Arwen and Uncle Albie, and my sister, tell her I love her.

Your Dave forever

A million kisses, a million wishes

XXXXXXXXXXXXXXXXXXXXXXXXXXXXXXXXXXXXXXXXXXXXXXXXXXXX

I give up on question one, this is going nowhere. Delyth crossed her arms, looked me straight in the eye and said "He's dead, Arwen!"

What was his last day with you like?

Just an ordinary Saturday, he went to work, she went to town to get mushrooms because it was beef stroganoff day(!) turns out that Delyth has a sort of weekly menu, she is writing me out a copy of it, then Dai said he was popping into the Green Man to give someone a loft conversion quote. It was quite late, about 10 o clock, so Delyth watched tv and then went to bed, he definitely hadn't been drinking which she thought was strange as regulars in the pub said he was drunk when he got there.

What was he wearing?

His normal clothes, navy tee-shirt, that weird jumper that you bought him with diamonds all over the front, jeans, trainers. *(I did not buy him that jumper, his mother bought it for him! I know I`m not a fashion expert but I`m not that bad. Fuming!)*

Did he take anything with him?

The police found a bag on the Head containing his wallet and his trainers, held down with a house brick, but as far as Delyth knew, he was empty handed when he left the house.

Any other information?

a) Delyth`s letter

b) She thought he came home about 11.30 but when she called out there was no answer.

c) He had been selling off his stuff at the car boot in Neath for the last few Saturdays because the business was in trouble, wouldn't let her go with him, said she would be bored and it was too cold for her.

d) A postcard was found in his van; it was a view of a golden sunset reflecting on the sea and on the back was written

My Darling Johnny,

It`s lovely down here, can`t wait for you to join me

Love you forever and ever and ever

Frankie xxxxxxxxx

She has no idea who Frankie and Johnny are.

The police told her that people disappear for all sorts of reasons but the fact that he left his van behind was telling. She didn't know what telling meant, neither do I, does it mean he left it behind because he was dead or because he didn't need it anymore but was still alive? I told Delyth about the article I had read about people going missing.

She just repeated her, "He`s dead, Arwen!" mantra. I need to ask Police Officer Carys what telling means. "Is that it?" I ask finally, she looks a bit shamefaced and squirmy but said, "Yes, that's it Arwen," she is lying!

Facts

1. *Disappeared in January 2018 at 11pm approximately*
2. *No body*
3. *Sold important and treasured possessions prior to disappearing*
4. *Left his van outside the bungalow with keys in it*
5. *Left three notes but all with ambiguous wording*
6. *Police not bothered*

Friday 25th January *St Dwynwen`s Day*

1pm

Dai`s birthday, he would be (or *is* if my intuition is correct) 51years old. I feel it in my bones that he has run away. I wonder if he still has his DIY tattoo? that would be a distinguishing mark on his body wouldn`t it? It`s on his left arm, obviously, as he is right handed, I might phone the police station and update their info for them, I don`t expect Delyth remembered, mostly because he covered it up with a plaster when he left me, I told him, you can cover it up Dai, but plasters fall off all the time, and every time one falls off, you will see

to remind you what a despicable adulterer and a useless tattooist you are!

February

Take a leap of faith

Intentions

Go out more

Be nicer

Be more interesting

Find a new job

Get a boyfriend

Find a new hobby

Be a better daughter

Be a better auntie

Write longer poems

Find out what really happened to Dai.

I have signed up to the Lottery and decided not to give up smoking this year. Yay! So, I've crossed them off the list. Uncle Albie has found his own carer, so crossed that off as well.

Friday 1st February

Phone Police Officer Carys

Find a box

11pm

Betty Upstairs was putting out a big box for the recycling, so I asked her if I could have it, "Of course you can my lovely" she said. Now I will have to put up with her enquiring about the box, I should have just waited for her to go back upstairs and then nicked it.

Phoned Carys to ask if Dai`s tattoo was a distinguishing mark, she says she will log it on the database. I said, "Are you ok Carys?" She said, "Perhaps he isn't dead but is just missing and doesn't want to be found, that`s his business." Weird, Carys could have just inadvertently given me the confirmation I am looking for, ***he has buggered off and is not dead.*** She doesn't know what telling means either, she said it`s just a saying.

My hair should have grown about half an inch now, meaning it`s about two inches long, which sounds a lot but isn`t. Faye from across the road popped into work to see me, "Here" she said, holding out a very old carrier bag "It`s a wig, used to be Beryl`s" I was shocked! "As in used to be Beryl`s before she died? And, I seem to remember you saying you took it to the undertakers for her to wear at the fucking viewings!"

"Anyway I`m not wearing a bastard wig, I`ll look like one of the Witches"

"What witches?"

"The Witches from the Witches!"

Rhiannon texted reminding me to meet them tomorrow at the Green Man, she suggested I bring a flower or a bio-degradable heart to throw over the headland, but that it`s not necessary.

Sunday 3rd February – *Yorkshire Pudding Day*

Meet others outside the Green Man at 10.45am

11pm

Dai jumped into the sea a year ago, we never found his body, in spite of people saying knowingly that the sea always brings them home. Rhiannon and Mam and Dad Davies were devastated. In the weeks that followed we all held our breath, waiting for news, but none came. We are going up to the Headland today at 11am, which is 12 hours earlier than we think he jumped, but I refused to go up there in the dark.

As far as we can tell, he left the pub quite drunk according to the bar staff at 10.45pm after loud mutterings and loads of intense and long cwtches for the women, saying things like "Take care mate" and "Don`t be like me" and was last seen trudging up the hill to the Cerrig-Mor Head, carrying a brick or something. Gwyn Bears, who spoke to him to ask what he was doing, was told, "What I should have done years ago mate." I asked Gwyn what happened next and he said, "I dunno, went home mun!"

The last I heard of him was a handwritten note posted through my door, it was waiting for me the next morning. I found it on the door mat after Delyth's frantic phone call at 8am and before PC Donald Davies (no relation) turned up to question me, in a very accusatory manner if you ask me.

The police gave me the note back after they had finished with it.

Dear Arwen,

Sorry it has come to this, I am going to a happier place. Please look after Rhiannon, Uncle Albie, and Delyth for me. You can keep my vinyl collection

Dai x

His vinyl collection! About 10 LPs, all bought at car boots! His favourites were "Max Boyce, Live at Treorchy" and Simon and Garfunkel "Bridge over troubled water" which he had to borrow a pound off me for, so technically it's mine anyway as I don't remember him giving me the pound back.

We left Albie and Mam in the pub while me, Delyth, Rhiannon and Richard, Owen, Police Officer

Carys, and Dai`s best friend Badger traipsed up to the Head from where Dai had jumped into the sea. Rhiannon was holding a white rose, I asked her if she was ok, she had been crying, her eyes were puffy and she said all she could think of was how Dai had turned up at her house the Friday before he went missing with a £20 note for Owen and 2 bottles of wine. They had sat around the table and Rhiannon had asked him if he was alright, he had held her hand and said, I`ll always love you little sister, never forget that. I asked if she thought this was a bit weird, but she hadn't at the time, it was just Dai being Dai.

Delyth was carrying a small blue carrier bag and was all in black. When we got to the top, she shouted "Fly high Dai, we love you!" turned the bag upside down shook out a load of grey lumpy dust in the general direction of the sea. "What the fuck!" said Rhiannon clutching her rose to her chest as if to protect it from the mess now swirling over the grass at the edge of the Head. "When you said you were bringing something, I thought you meant flowers!" Which means that whatever was happening was unexpected, Rhiannon never uses the f word. Owen thought the whole thing was hilarious and was covertly taking photos on his birthday iPhone.

Turns out, Delyth had mixed a load of chalk dust (Giant White pavement chalks are best, we found out later, when someone asked her) fag ash and the dust from the vacuum cleaner into pretend ashes for Dai! "It`s still got little filters in it" I said

"Yes" she said, "That`s to make it more lifelike, bits of bones, you know."

"And it has 2 gold rings in it Delyth, fake are they?" I asked innocently.

She smiled, "Yes, well we would have been married if you had signed the papers Arwen." That was a lie, as Dai and I never discussed divorce, but I let it go, just looked smug and smiled conspiratorially at Rhiannon instead, she gave me a wink and a thumbs up, which I assume was because I was being all dignified about things, in spite of the plastic rings quip.

Richard, not known for his wit, so not sure if he was being funny, said "At least the Vacuum dust might have a bit of Dai in it like." Looking shocked, Rhiannon said "Implying that until today Delyth hasn`t cleaned her bungalow or needed to empty the bag in the last year!" Delyth looked miffed and mortified all at once.

Carys cleared her throat loudly "I could do you for littering mind Delyth, have you any idea how long these plastic rings and fag end filters take to decompose?"

I upset everyone not already upset by the pantomime enacted by Delyth, by saying "He is not dead anyway, I feel it in my bones, the police, (I shot an accusing look at Carys) did a rubbish investigation, that's why I am doing my own!" They all gave me pitying looks, then we went to the pub.

Later I caught Rhiannon and Delyth in the toilet with police officer Carys, Delyth was saying, "She is obsessed with Dai, she won`t let things go, I`m trying to move on with my life"

"Don`t mind me" I said, barging my way through them to the nearest cubicle and slamming the door shut.

Rhiannon said "We are worried about you love" I shouted "HE IS NOT DEAD, and I will prove it to you, and if moving on with your life means hanging out in the Spar waiting for your ex to come out of the storeroom, then, yes Delyth, you are moving on!" There was complete silence and when I crept out of the toilet, the outer bit was empty, so no idea if they heard what I said. I went back to the table, they were all watching me warily so I said "Sorry, a bit stressed at the moment, with my hair and everything" that sorted it, there is no denying that my hair is still awful.

Later, Rhiannon said, "You have to stop using your hair as an excuse my lovely, it looks gorgeous now" I gave her a cwtch, "He is not dead Rhiannon and according to my calculations, my hair which grows at approximately ½ inch a month has grown by less than ½ an inch, which makes my hair 2 inches long" I stopped talking and glared at her for a bit instead, she had nothing more to say about it.

After lunch in the pub, I drove Albie up to Rhiannon's for board games. When we got there I could hear the unmistakable bray that was Delyth's laughter. She and Mam were side by side on the settee looking at photos of Owen's Christening Party. Apparently (and conveniently for the adults not wishing to offend me, in my opinion) they had all stayed silent when Owen had innocently invited her back for scrabble, Rhiannon whispered that she didn`t like to uninvite her, and added, "We are all a sort of family Arwen, think about it and she is not an evil person, just a very stupid one" I can`t stay mad at Rhiannon and she is right, we are all family. Not boasting but I am brilliant at scrabble! Delyth is spectacularly bad at it, well you can't have everything, can you! I am very good at board games, all Delyth has are cookery skills, the ability to walk in stilettos and long blonde hair.

Wednesday 6th February

11pm

Write letter of resignation to Geoff (Don`t send it yet, get the job first)

Google how to appear less boring at job interviews

Email from chemists to say I have an interview on Friday, goodbye Geoff Norman, hello new improved life! (If I get the job, that is.) I quite like the idea of working in the chemist shop. They have really cool white uniforms like the doctors in American soaps wear.

Hopefully, they do staff discounts as well. I could save a fortune on shower gel etc.

Went to poetry group, I read my very short poem about Dai not being dead.

I listen to reason

Participate in the wringing of hands

The wearing of black

The wails of grief in the darkness

But I know you`re not dead

Of us all, I alone know that, and I alone will find you

And bring you home.

I think everyone is fed up with Leonards extremely long poems, which this week was about the finding of America by the Welsh, entitled "The saga of the new Celtic lands" so we have decided to give haikus a go for a bit, thank God for that!

I've been thinking about how obsessed I am with Dai. I was always a bit in awe of him to be honest, Rhianon's big brother, always acting so grown up and cool. He was always nice to me as well when I was growing up. When Dad died, he looked after the business and Mam until I could move home for good. I don't think I love him anymore, I'm just not convinced that he is dead. That's what it is I think, that's why I'm obsessed with finding out what really happened to him.

Thursday 7th February

8am

Yay, email off the Lottery to say I won £30 on last night's draw! I was hoping for a bit more, a couple of million would do me fine. Read about this woman the other day who won millions on the lottery, she said she was going to keep her job in the local sandwich shop. If I won the lottery the first thing I'd do is call Geoff, tell him I hate him and resign with immediate effect! I'd buy a lovely cottage by the sea on the Llyn Peninsula, another one somewhere in Cornwall, then I'd give everyone I love loads of money to buy houses with, buy a posh seafront house here, and a nice car then I'd work out how much money I would need to live on until I was say a hundred, and give the rest away, maybe.

So! Life is looking up, won the lottery, and my hair definitely looks longer, I no longer look like an aged skinhead girl, the upside to being scalped is that I am going to save loads of money because I won't need a haircut for months! Bastard Carrie!

Friday 8th February

11pm

Had my interview at the chemists, a teenage boy from Cardiff with acne said he was the assistant HR manager. He thought my application was very interesting (w**ker).

After the interview when it was clear I wasn`t going to get the job, he puts on a sad face, points at my hair, and says,

"Just like my grandma"

I take a moment to work out whether his implication that I am recovering from cancer might be advantageous, decided it wouldn't be but I`ll give it a go anyway, I break into a smile and say

"Can I have the job then? It might not be for long! Wink wink!"

I handed him my business card as he ushered me out the door,

"How is your gran, anyway"

"She`s dead" he said, "The chemo didn`t work."

I feel bloody awful about it, everyone thinks I`m nice except Mam who says I have turned into a horrible bitter person since Dai left, I think she is right for once. Instead of going home, I bought a cappuccino and went and sat on the sea wall, it was bloody freezing there. A vaguely familiar man passed by. He was walking really close to the water line. My heart leapt because for a second he turned and looked at me and waved and he was the image of Ross Poldark with short hair from a distance, I waved back. His face rings a bell, not just because he looks like Ross, made me feel as if life was worth living for some reason, in spite of me being a horrible person.

When I told Mam how I`m probably not going to get the chemist`s job, she said she was relieved because her ex-friend`s daughter Chantelle works there and she had told this ex-friend that I was something high up in the council, so me working in a shop would be a bit of a come down for her. With Mam, it`s all about Mam.

Saturday 9th February

Scrap the letter of resignation

Look for another job

Think about expanding the bookmark business

Check out other stall holders for ideas

Spruce up CV

Google how to encourage hair growth

11pm

Another really quiet day at the craft fair, bought some home-made plum jam though, it`s lush!

The usual moans about whether or not we should forget January and February craft fairs. We should have a proper meeting and take a vote on it to be honest. Or I could just send Si around with a clipboard and a pen and conduct a straw poll.

This evening thought of clearing the desk, looked at it, moved some of the old papers onto the bed and put the box on the desk, then gave up and watched "The Vikings" instead. Why am I so attracted to marauding Scandinavian warriors wearing loads of fur and feathers and eating whole chickens for lunch?

Sunday 10th February

11pm

We are not playing Scrabble after Sunday lunch anymore because I take it too seriously and everyone is complaining about my obscure words and the time it takes to look them up, but that`s ok because I`ve discovered that I`m brilliant at Boggle, teamed up with Owen and his friends, and we beat them all!!

Wednesday 13th February

11pm

Popped into Uncle Albie`s, he is fine. Ken has introduced Albie to themed evenings, Wednesday evening is poker and chips, as in Ken nips to the chip shop for sausage specials, then they play poker for chips, Ken`s a bit weird, but harmless enough.

St Valentine`s day is tomorrow. He is the English version of St Dwynwen, *she* is the legendary daughter of a King, Brychan Byrcheiniog and was a fifth century Princess whose tragic love life led her to dedicate her life to God and lovers everywhere. One of her famous sayings was "Nothing wins hearts like cheerfulness". Dwynwen had fallen in love with Maelon, and wanted to marry him, but her father said no and so she fled asking God for help. An angel appeared to her and gave her a potion that would help her fall out of love with Maelon, but when she drank the potion, Maelon turned into a block of ice. God then relented and granted her three wishes. The first was that Maelon would be released from the spell, the second was that God would help all true lovers and a third was that she would never have to marry, to this end she dedicated the rest of her life to God, became a nun, retreated to North Wales, and lived in religious deprivation and pious solitude. I expect quite a lot of praying and a lack of food was involved.

Saint Valentine lived in the 3rd Century, he was a Roman and was beheaded on the 14th of February. Legend has it that he befriended his jailors daughter and left her a note which was found after his death saying

"From your Valentine," he is also the patron saint of bees and epilepsy. I prefer St Dwynwen, to be honest.

Thursday 14th February *St Valentine`s Day*

7pm

Going to a Valentine`s Day dance this evening at Ty Mawr, you never know, I might meet the love of my life and that will make up for no Valentine`s cards

1am

Back home, it`s really late, but I`m tamping and need to vent! Apparently, according to Glenda, I look like a bald married librarian, and that`s why I haven't met anyone since Dai left, and she shouted, "Who the hell wears a cardigan to a dance?" as we walked through the car park which cheered up the gang of drunken people behind us no end if their loud laughs and rude comments were anything to go by. Off to bed, I`m never going to speak to her or go out with her again!!

Friday 15th February

11pm

I`m still tamping about Glenda ranting about me looking like a bald librarian! I know she was really drunk but it`s still not on! I phoned her this morning and asked her for an explanation and said it`s not my fault I`ve been scalped! She said that personally she wouldn't leave the house to go to the Spar looking like that, let alone a Valentine`s dance. I said, "Oh carry on with the criticism Glenda, don`t mind me! Oh, and by the way, I'm recording you on my phone, so I can play back what you've said when you want to know why I`m not speaking to you."

She shouted, "For fucks sake!" and hung up. She is lucky I`m at work and not standing next to her!

Went to Mam`s as usual, I was still a bit grumpy and as she walked me to the front door and handed me my coat and bag I asked her if I looked like a bald librarian. I`ll never learn. She was still laughing loudly, leaning on the door frame as I made my way down the garden path, although she never actually answered the question. I'm glad she finds a bit of fucking jollity in my disastrous life.

Taking advantage of not having to write in Journal every day and having time off. My life is rubbish, not worth the ink. Embracing my boring-ness with a vengeance.

Tuesday 19th February

11pm

Saw Glenda outside Greggs this morning, forgot I wasn't speaking to her so said "Hiya" before I remembered and started fuming again but then she said sorry and bought me a cappuccino and a bacon and cheese thing so I knew that she meant it, Glenda is so tight. Anyway, we are going to try out the weekly Singles Nite! at Ty Mawr and find ourselves loads of nice men. I have promised not to wear cardigans.

Tuesday 26th February

11pm

Finally finished asking my friends, family, and random acquaintances if I have turned into a bitter old woman, here are the results, they are not very encouraging to be honest.

Question – Have I turned into a bitter old woman?

Answers

Si – yes.

Faye – just more grumpy.

My Boss – haven't really noticed.

Mam – yes.

Shirley – for god`s sake, get a life!

Dianne – no, I don`t know, maybe it`s the perimenopause (Dianne is in the menopause stage of her life at last and is now an expert at diagnosing it)

Glenda – a bit.

Dave next door – a bit down like.

Ron the milk – nah, you're fine mun!

Rhiannon – a bit depressed my love, your worst self.

Richard – what Rhiannon said, absolutely your worst self!

Owen – you cry more (Do I?)

Betty Upstairs – no, not really. How is the box?

Jackie from the chip shop – had moved on to next customer, it was very busy there.

Uncle Albie – no more than normal.

Les from the Spar – he said it was only when I talk about Delyth (His cheating ex-girlfriend) I shouldn't have asked him really, he is quite open to Delyth's attempts at reconciliation at the moment, and I just remind him of her affair with Dai when he sees me, poor sod, maybe I should give the Spar a miss for a bit.

Mixed reactions to my question then but on the whole the answer is yes, and that is another reason why I can't teach the meditation classes anymore. (Bit relieved really, bloody quite stressful, teaching complex meditation techniques, especially when the people at the back pretend they can't hear what you are saying and carry on with their gossiping about that woman who ran away with the traffic warden).

Thursday 28th February

Find some interesting friends

Stop being bitter

11pm

Tomorrow is not a leap year day, if it was I would ask someone to marry me after we have established that Dai is either dead or divorceable. I can`t think of anyone at the moment, although my Ross look alike is definitely a possibility once I have stopped looking like a bald librarian. My hair should now be two and a half inches long.

Darren up the road was proposed to on a leap year, he was going out with this girl from the Rhondda, he only said yes because he didn't want to upset her, but unknown to him, she had been planning it for months. She whipped out two rings and a date for the wedding, it was all signed and sealed for within a couple of months and she had moved into his house. I see him in town sometimes, he still looks a bit shocked! And overfed. Yeah, shocked and overfed. The next leap Year is in 2020, so I have got to get my skates on If I`m going to establish the facts surrounding Dai`s disappearance and my marital status and find someone to propose to.

Have looked up how to find interesting friends. Really good suggestions came up, one was "Join a social group," looked that up and the definition is, "Two or more people who interact on the basis of mutual expectations and who share a common identity." So basically you only need two people to be a group? In that case I am probably a member of quite a few social groups.

The Si and Arwen moaning about Geoff group.

The Rhiannon and Arwen coffee at Luigi`s group.

The Mam and Arwen Fish and Chips Friday Club.

I can think of loads more, but I`m tired now, and it`s St David`s Day tomorrow, so I need to get up early and find my daffodil brooch that Mam crocheted for me.

March

Take care of the little things

<u>*Intentions*</u>

Go out more

Be nicer

Be more interesting

Find a new job

Get a boyfriend

Find a new hobby

Be a better daughter

Be a better auntie

Write longer poems

Find out what really happened to Dai.

Friday 1ˢᵗ March *St David`s Day*

Buy daffodils and Welsh cakes for the front desk

Set up a display in the foyer

Make a fucking daily bookmark!!

Find another job

Nothing to cross off my list this time, I`ll have to try harder. Going out more is probably the easiest to do. Although after the disaster of St Valentine and the cardigan, that`s a bit daunting at the moment, I`m not very good at going out. We will see how Singles Nite! pans out.

11pm

When I got to work after buying the Welsh cakes and daffodils, Si had already made the St David's day display on the table in the foyer. I fetched a plate and a vase from the kitchen and was just setting them up when Geoff emerged from the toilets.

"Ooh Welsh cakes! Lovely I`ll just have two, thankyou Arwen."

Si and I just glared at him because last year we both had a lecture about wasting public money on sentimental claptrap and he said he hated Welsh cakes.

Delyth posted her weekly menu through my door, and looking through it, it`s probably one of the reasons Dai left me, he liked his food, but to be fair to me, I work and look after my mother and Uncle Albie, all Delyth does is knit baby pastel pink and baby blue cot blankets, (Rhiannon said I am fucking mean to criticise her for that, because she lost a baby when she was in her twenties, and me, of all people, should understand, I hate it when Rhiannon gives me a telling off.) Anyway, Delyth knits for premature babies, potters around the huge bungalow her mother left her, and cooks gourmet meals for philandering carpenters, if her weekly menu is anything to go by.

Delyth`s weekly menu

Monday   *Cottage pie with chips and vegetables, fruit salad and ice cream*

Tuesday   *Chicken chasseur with mashed potatoes and green beans, apple tart and custard*

Wednesday	*Spaghetti bolognaise with garlic bread, Italian fruit cake*
Thursday	*Steak and chips with salad, yoghurt, and fruit*
Friday	*Picky Eats and film night*
Saturday	*Beef stroganoff with rhubarb crumble*
Sunday	*Roast dinner with all the trimmings*

Arwen. All recipes available on google xx

I googled "Picky eats" no results that made any sense, I'll ask her on Sunday since she has totally ingratiated herself with my family and is now a regular Sunday Luncher. To be fair, she turns up with amazing afters, which spurs Mam on to be more creative with our Friday night deserts, we had apple crumble with vanilla ice cream tonight! Lush!

Mam a bit sad today because this is the day 40 years ago that her mother died, I always take her a huge bunch of daffodils and then we look through the photo albums while sharing stories of my grandmother, we have a little cry and she always says, "I still think about her every day, still miss her". Although I was very young, I remember her last words to me. I was wearing my St David`s day costume and had gone into her room to say good morning. There she was, as usual, sitting up in bed wearing her lilac bed jacket, her gnarly old hands resting on the patchwork blanket. The stereotypical image of an old nanna, smiling sweetly at me. She gave me a big cwtch and said "You look fucking silly in that hat, cariad; take it off quick and I`ll hide it under my pillow." I know she meant no harm, but her words are seared into my soul, I`ll never be able to wear any sort of hat without feeling very fucking silly.

I think that`s why I was a rubbish Brownie, always turning up without my little brown beret and getting into trouble with Akela.

Saturday 2nd March

Craft fair

11pm

Lynda who knits bobble hats and scarves and sells them at the craft fair came over to my table and whispered, "Can I have your advice Arwen?" Turns out Ninja, Cerrig-Mor`s very own criminal, asked her to knit him a "Black Barraclava" I bit my tongue and didn't correct her pronunciation although that pedantic bore who lives inside my head kept saying "Balaclava" and was desperate to take over my mouth, in the end I had to give in and say, "*Can* you knit Ba-la-cla-vas Lynda?" she didn't flinch, just said she was sure she could, but was just very concerned that she would be responsible for any increase in his criminal activity. I just told her to take his money in advance and then talk to Police Officer Carys about it. She was very pleased with my guidance; how come I give good advice to other people but never give myself good advice?

I think I am getting better at controlling my compulsion to correct people's pronunciation and bad grammar, I mean to be fair, these people have done me no real harm. Either that or I have given up caring, if I keep it up, I might be able to cross "Be nicer" off my list of intentions, especially if I curb myself when I'm online.

Mind you, "Bert from Risca" I would *never* buy a chest of drawers from a person who thinks it is spelt chester draws! No matter how much you verbally abuse me when I point out your error!

!!Singles Nite!!

At Ty Mawr

8 `Till Late (midnight)

Smart clothes only Entry £5

Come along, dance, and look for the love of your life

If you are coming on your own for the first time and would like Sanjeev or Sharon to meet you in the foyer, just message us on **Facebook**

Or carry a pink flower

Sunday 3rd March

7pm

Lovely lunch at Rhiannon's, had a quick search through her wardrobe and we found a lush black dress from her thin days which fits me, so I`ve borrowed that for a bit. I`m a bit worried about Singles Nite! I can`t stop thinking about bald librarians, I actually had a dream last night where I was wearing the wig that Faye offered me, a pink cardigan, and nothing else at all! Glenda popped into my dream and said in a very nasty voice, "I hope you are not going to the Spar looking like that."

Oh yes, picky eats are finger foods! Ridiculous.

12.30am

It`s half past midnight, I`ve been to Singles Nite! Quite exciting, I am treating tonight's outing as an information gathering exercise. We are definitely going again next week. If I want to fit in a bit more I need to up my game, higher heels, more lipstick, and I definitely need a few sparkly tops and black trousers. Everyone looked very well dressed, even the men had made a massive effort. The music was great and the DJ takes requests, I`m going to make a list of my favourite songs and keep it in the sparkly little handbag I`m going to buy. I danced all night and even if I say so myself, I`m quite good at it. Sanjeev and Sharon are very glamourous and are also amazing dancers, the night begins with them doing a couple of tangos, first they dance together, then they drag two random people onto the dance floor and do a tango with them. I hid behind the big bloke wearing a multicoloured waistcoat when they were scouting for partners.

Shattered now!

Monday 4th March

11pm

The mystery of the man from the beach is solved! I spotted him in the Co-op today, and I remembered how I knew him, it's Dai the Death and he definitely looks like Ross Poldark now that he has grown up, gone are the braces and the funny little moustache he was trying to grow. He was wearing a long grey parka and was buying a pasta bake ready meal. I boldly went up to him.

"Hiya! Remember me! A level geography? The girl with the orange crocheted pencil case?"

"Hiya Arwen, saw you on the beach wall the other day, you ok?"

"Yeah, living the life Dai."

He looked a bit miffed at that and said he had to go. I was disappointed but then Dai the Death was always a bit weird, who wouldn`t be if your dad was the town undertaker, but who would have thought he would turn out to be such a Ross lookalike! I wonder what he`s up to? I thought he had moved away.

Wednesday 6th March

11pm

Attempted my first Haiku for poetry group.

Searching for you still

Where the sun dies in the west

Sadness bourne aloft by sorrowing birds

Loads of criticism because the last line has too many syllables, I know that! Next time its anything we want because loads of people found haikus hard. I like them because they are very short and quite profound if you ask me. Also, if I get really good at them and just compose haikus, I can cross "Write longer poems" off my list, because they are definitely not meant to be long.

Thursday 7th March

Fix the haiku asap

11pm

I had to help this very disabled lady today, she was going to the "Art in the Community." The class was up on the first floor in the "Princess Diana" workshop, she had one of those disabled scooters and I had to help her get into the lift, it was a bit of a tight squeeze.

I had to get her in, press the floor button and then run up the stairs to help her out, a bit breathless by the time I got there. Anyway I was thinking, she was much younger than me and here she was, state of the art purple scooter, disability living allowance, doesn't have to work, off to the art class for a relaxing hour painting kittens or something similar. I, on the other hand, had to go back to the office, book purple scooter lady a taxi with a ramp to get her home, go to the kitchen and wash up after the Russian classes and clean the kitchen in time for the "Happy Singing" group, (they are so nice to be honest, can't sing very well but they do enjoy it) before heading back up to the Princess Diana suite to help get purple scooter lady back into the lift for the taxi home. I was exhausted by the time her taxi arrived!

I never thought I would be feeling envious of people who can`t walk and have to get help to get into a lift.

If people could see inside my head they would never speak to me again.

Sunday 10th March

Kindly tell Derrick about Singles Nite! Be clear you are not inviting him to sit at your table or spend the evening with you!!!!!!

My music list

1. *Meatloaf-Anything for love*

2. *Dire Straits-Romeo and Juliet*

3. *Meat Loaf-Heaven can wait*

4. *Dire Straits-Brothers in arms*

5. *Meatloaf -Paradise by the Dashboard light*

6. *Meatloaf-Dead ringer for love*

7. *Queen-Love of my life*

8. *Adele- Someone like you*

9. *Rod Stewart-Handbags and Gladrags*

10. *Rod Stewart-Reason to Believe*

11. *Rod Stewart-Maggie May*

12. *REM-Everybody hurts*

13. *Meatloaf-Two out of three ain`t bad*

14. *Aerosmith-Don`t want to miss a thing*

15. *Meatloaf-I`d lie for you*

16. *Meatloaf-You took the words*

I can think of loads more but you have to stop somewhere.

7pm

Lunch at Rhiannon's, then went home to get ready for the evening at Ty Mawr!

1am

Lovely night dancing, only spoiled by the fact that the DJ lost my list! I promised to write him out a new one, he said he couldn`t wait.

Glenda told the DJ that it was my birthday tomorrow, so he played "Happy Birthday To You" and everyone joined in. Derrick bought me half a lager and offered to dance with me, I didn`t want to dance with him but thought it would be rude to refuse. The trouble with Derrick is that he thinks he is a bit of a catch, I wish I had *his* confidence.

Monday 11th March. *Our birthdays!*

Buy birthday buns for work

Rhiannon`s for cake at 6 (Pick up Mam and Albie)

11pm

It is forty five plus years since, according to our mothers, Rhiannon and I bonded in the baby clinic when we were both in the queue for a jab. Our lives have been entwined ever since and I don`t know about her, but I am so glad about that! Our mothers have ruthlessly exploited the fact that we had the same birthday, as it saved a lot when it came to parties etc.

Delyth outdid herself on the gift front again. The package she gave me held a framed photo of me, her and Dai and a tin of homemade biscuits. That woman is completely insensitive. I`ve put the photo in the birthday box under the Boots bubble bath from the Secret Santa 2014, and ate *all* the biscuits while fuming about where the framed photo could have come from?

To be fair, I`ve bought loads of rubbish presents in my time. The one that haunts me whenever I pass an Oxfam shop was the light-up singing snowman I bought for Alvira in their pre-Christmas sale, she was so annoyed with me! It finished off our friendship. The last time I saw her was when she went out of her way to bring the singing snowman into the community centre as a prize for the quiz night raffle, making sure I noticed it as she exclaimed, "This is a bit tasteless but some child might like it." So I admit I`m not great at choosing presents for people, but not as bad as Delyth or that woman I used to work with who sent a photo of the grave diggers filling in her husband`s grave, to his mistress for her birthday. It wasn`t even a very good photo. Although to be fair, that was probably a blessing.

Wednesday 13th March

11pm

I`ve bought a pair of walking boots out of Mam`s birthday money! A bit of an impulse buy but nicer than make-up or a year's supply of soap, I can wear them when walking down on the beach, or even just sitting on the sea wall watching the world go by…maybe a pair of binoculars would have been a better buy, I could use them to spot my lovely man Dai the Death coming from miles away and think of something interesting to say as I jump down onto the beach off the sea wall…safely of course, that goes without saying, this is not a bloody Jane Austin novel. I`ll ask Richard if he has any binoculars, I'll tell him it`s for birdwatching.

Sunday 17th March

6.30pm

Been to Rhiannon's for lunch and now getting ready for Singles Nite!

I asked Delyth about the birthday photo, she said it was from the charity garden party at the community centre a couple of years ago. On behalf of the centre, I had put a call out for amateur photographers to document the event and practise their photography skills, her next-door neighbour responded and brought Delyth along because he was a bit shy. When I was mingling and Dai was at the buffet table helping himself to free food, Delyth commented on the mis-shaped gingerbread men, they got talking about her love of cookery, his love of food, and how she wishes she had an island in her kitchen, he offered to give her a quote and the rest is history. Delyth said Dai fell in love with her while munching her bacon and egg baps, which she liked to cook for him when he was constructing her island. So basically it is my fault that Dai ran off with her. Grrrr! (And whoever made the mis-shaped gingerbread men!) I said she could have the photo back as it obviously means a lot to her but she replied, "Oh, bless you Arwen! I have the original photo in a very similar frame to the one I gave you!" I hate her.

1am

Back from Singles Nite! I gave the DJ another music list, he promised to put it in a safe place and played Meatloaf, "Two out of three ain't bad." Happy now and very tired.

Tuesday 19th March

11pm

I have started sorting out my clothes into three piles, charity, wearing and not wearing. So, tonight I will have to sleep on the settee because the bedroom looks as if a bomb has exploded in the wardrobe and has scattered clothes all over the bed, floor, and ironing board. Which I put up so that I would have somewhere to put socks and underwear. I have thirty-seven pairs of socks and five odd ones. How come? Calculated that I probably never need to buy another pair as long as I live. I think I should recycle them, I could just keep fourteen pair and get rid of the rest, that's a whole drawer freed up!

I like sleeping on the settee, I could sleep in the spare room/study but the bed and the desk are still piled high with all the old paperwork I haven't got around to sorting through. Betty Upstairs' box is still empty and waiting, so cwtching up now, with my duvet, to watch the rolling news.

Saturday 23rd March

11pm

Really weird interaction at the craft fair with a very big lady with tattoos and black leggings about my innovative idea to give prospective customers a template of a bookmark, to design and colour in.

She marches over to my table, "Iya, can I have one of these and a borrow of a pen?"

"Yes of course," I say, she turns it to the blank side then she shouts over to Mandy (Handmade Soap), opposite.

"Mand! what`s her name again?"

"Mary Lee Hansward" says Mandy, "she`s on Facebook, long black hair, works in the Rusty Anchor in the kitchens, stunner mind! Way out of your Anthony`s league, to be fair."

"Ta love" says big lady then turns to me, how do you spell Hansward?

I clear my throat and spell it for her and then I ask her if she is going to order a bespoke bookmark, "A what?" I point to the sign propped up against my cash box and I explain that she can write her own message on it etc, simple concept really and then I'll make it for her. She scrutinised the sign.

"How much," she says,

"£2 or two for £3" I say.

"I haven't got any colouring pencils "she said,

"Well," I say, "Do it in biro and let me choose the colours."

"Nah," she says.

Scary lady turns to go then instead looks glaringly at me and says

"Haven't you got any pencils?"

"No," I say, "didn't bring any,"

"Lost opportunity there love," she shakes her head and points to the café area,

"People could fill them in over there, nice cup of tea and a bit of colouring in"

I`m so impressed, that I asked Nigel Next Table if I can borrow a few of his colouring pencils, £2 For 6, he says. I give him two pound and hand them over to my customer, she picks up two more templates and heads off for a coffee.

As I`m packing up, she comes back over, gives me the pencils back and says she will have two bookmarks for £3, I tell her she has to pay in advance, she gives me a stony grimace, but I`m not intimidated so she hunts in her rucksack for her purse. Olivia (I`m assuming that`s her name) hands me three pound coins, I thank her much too ingratiatingly and put the commissions in the folder, I want to get to the co-op before I starve to death.

"See you next Saturday" I say, she just glares a bit more and marches off.

Found myself searching for Dai the Death in the ready meals aisle, but he wasn't there. Tried to remember what Delyth cooks on Saturday, gave up and bought a half price carbonara, 2 Portuguese tarts, and some vegetables for tomorrow instead. Messaged Rhiannon to see if she wanted some out of date bread for the freezer, she didn't want any, even though it was the artisan stuff, with olives and dried tomatoes. I bought a loaf for my freezer.

Sunday 24th March

7pm

Took a quick look at Olivia's templates today, the first one is lovely, all flowers and I love you Mam, second one says, "I fucking hate you Tony, you are a Tw*t. BTW Mary Lee is a tart."

1am

Substitute DJ at Singles Nite! Doesn't know anything about a list. Proper DJ has gone to Portugal and can't be contacted apparently. Totally unprofessional!

Monday 25th March

11pm

Went to work at 8.30, tested fire alarms after warning Lizzie that they were being tested as she panics otherwise and runs around shouting "Fire! Fire" and going back to her cleaning stuff cupboard to get her handbag even though I have pointed out to her on numerous occasions that she shouldn`t do that. Finished off invoices. Washed up dishes from meetings last night and cleaned up kitchen. Set up three rooms for various groups, pulled a muscle in my rib cage again! Can`t complain about it or wince even, as I need the job. Definitely going to look for another one where they pay me properly and value my contribution. Finished exactly on time, and didn`t bother to wash cups up after the Coffee and a Chat group who over-run as usual. What the hell do they find to talk about every bloody Monday anyway?

Friday 29th March *Mam`s Birthday*

Chicken not fish

11pm

Called into Uncle Albie`s to see if he was ok, Ken has gone away for a couple of days and I promised to check up on him and bring him food, then off to the chip shop for Mam`s chips, she splashed out and had a chicken leg and some gravy this week as it`s her birthday tea! I had bought a card, a very expensive chiffon scarf which she will turn her nose up at and stuff in a drawer and as an afterthought got her a journal like mine so that she can write her thoughts in it! Chose a purple one to match the scarf.

Surprise, surprise! She really liked the scarf but wasn't sure about the journal, said "Shame it's not a diary, with dates in, would have been much more useful, never mind."

I told her about Ken going away so I need to get food for Albie on the way home, and then gratefully accepted the big container of beef stew that she said I could have for him, to save me going to the shops. Also took the mince pies left over from Christmas even though I and Albie hate them, called in to his flat on the way back and gave him half of the beef stew, (I'm keeping the rest for my dinner tomorrow), and two mince pies. Got a lecture about how men need more food than women, gave him another mince pie to shut him up.

Because Mam is a brilliant cook, it is a constant source of dismay to her that I can't be bothered. She doesn't understand that I would rather die than spend more than half an hour in the kitchen after work. She blatantly lied to Cyril, him with the stinky kitchen, who had popped into Her's with a birthday card, by saying "Arwen's a very good cook"

Cyril (about 80, terrible teeth, stinky kitchen) looked at me with renewed interest "Oh aye" I said, "My ham sandwiches are famous" that cheered them both up. I am sure Mam would marry me off to anyone who asked if she had her way.

Saturday 30th March

11am

Because it's Mother's Day tomorrow, I completely sold out of nice bookmarks at the craft fair, those with "Mam" on them went first, had an argument with a horrible person who wanted to know why I couldn't turn her template into bookmark there and then, so I took a flowery one that was pre-made and very carefully wrote "Mam" on it in black felt tip, I thought she would give up, but no, she gave me the money, snatched the bookmark off me and marched away!

Sunday 31st March

Mother's day

Be nice to Mam

7pm

Mother's day, so Richard, Owen, and I did all the cooking and dishing up and later loaded the dishwasher. I gave Mam her card, a tinned luxury Dundee cake and a bottle of sherry. The card was very sentimental and because she loves all that, she insisted on reading it out to everyone, so then Rhiannon had to read Owen's card out as well, Albie sat there glowering and muttering "Bloody nonsense!" but we are used to that from the grumpy bitter old man so we ignored him.

1am

Went to singles night, the thing is, people come and go there, if they meet someone they drop out for a bit, so there are always newly single people turning up in their finery, some looking slightly desperate. A lot of them knew Dai and it is very interesting and also depressing to look at him from someone's else's perspective, especially when they are a bit tipsy and don't edit their views to spare my feelings. Main points to take away from these insights are

- *Bit of a bastard wasn't he*
- *Bit of a boy wasn't he (This means he was a bit of a bastard)*
- *You are better off without him love, even though I`m sorry he died like.*
- *He was always trying it on with me (Joan The Pop, Helen from Port Talbot, Julie Next door to Mam`s and numerous others, to many to mention)*

Derrick was there again, he is more confident now and fancies himself as a bit of a ladies man, he has his eyes on this smart but grumpy looking woman, they dance together quite a lot, even though she is playing hard to get. I don`t think Derrick will be on his own for long, tonight he refused a lift home in my car and later I saw him getting into the front passenger seat of Grumpy Woman`s red Corsa, Grumpy Woman`s friend protested loudly at this, she said "Oh, *I`ll* sit in the back then, is it Donna Marie?"

DJ should be back from his holidays next week, can`t wait, his substitute is very nice but only plays 1960`s stuff.

Can`t believe it`s the last day of March! Time to get on with my life! I have made no progress on the Dai problem either. I need some help, but the family just roll their eyes and try to distract me when I mention my doubts about him being dead.

April

Live, laugh, love

<u>*Intentions*</u>

Be nicer

Be more interesting

Find a new job

Get a boyfriend

Find a new hobby

Be a better daughter

Be a better auntie

Write longer poems

Find out what really happened to Dai.

Crossed going out more off the list as going out more.

Monday 1ˢᵗ April

11pm

Today being April Fool's day, I was prepared for the usual puerile tricks from Si, but instead, he looked really down, which is not like him at all. He finally admitted that his ex-girlfriend Megan is pregnant with twins and is demanding a shotgun wedding, she and her mam are coming around to his house tonight to have a chat with him and his mam, with a view to moving in as she has become homeless due to rats, and her mother said no way is she moving back home.

"Rats?" I ask, horrified.

"Yes, a pack of them living in the basement."

I check the time on the big wall clock behind us, it is 12.05 so I know it's not an April fool. I sit there speechless for a minute, then I leap into action! Taking a piece of paper and a pen, I turn to Si and say.

"Right! Let's make a to do list."

"April fool!" he shouts, "I put the clock on 10 minutes when you were checking the toilets!"

He is such an idiot, I have spent the whole morning worrying about him and trying to cheer him up with pasties and cream horns!

"Phew, glad that`s over," he says, "Epic that was!" I know that after Rhiannon, Si is my best friend, but I bloody hate him sometimes. He has refunded me the money for the cream horns but not the pasties.

Tuesday 2nd April

11pm

Started a list of people who might have an insight into Dai`s death/disappearance. I`m going to interview them to see if there are any clues we have missed.

Me (Obviously)

Si

Delyth

Les

Rhiannon

Richard

His best friend-Badger

Uncle Albie

Taxi driver

Workshop owner

Mam

I`ll try and get it done by the end of the month.

Wednesday 3rd April

11pm

Called into Uncle Albie`s, he seems fine, they were watching some weird film about the World War II and barely looked up to say hello, I think I can stop routinely checking up on him now and just carry on picking him up for Sunday lunch at Rhiannon`s. If anything bad is happening, he can tell us then. I`m more worried about Ken`s well-being to be honest, it must be a nightmare living with Albie.

I went to poetry group, read my poem about the Sky Goddess,

I dance along the rainbow road

Small planets, asteroids, and moonlets

Scuffed up by my bangled jangling feet

Skitter and scatter in my wake.

*My midnight gown sweeps up misty multicoloured
galaxies and clockwork solar systems*

They cling, still singing, still spinning, to my skirts

Twirling into their proper places, their preferred spaces

*A million small bright starlets make a twinkling circlet
above my head*

*A tiny crescent moon whirrs down like a tin toy and
settles on my brow*

*A small golden sun with a smiling face fixes itself to my
breast.*

*I laugh aloud at the joy of it all and stretch out my
arms.*

*Watching the chaos as my hands stir up the swirling
moonlit river of dust*

That flows eternally along the rainbow road.

No positive feedback, as usual. Barry asked what it was about, Laurence told him to shut up and said, "At least she tried, your contribution was a knock off, if you ask me!" I smiled gratefully at Laurence and passed him the plate of biscuits which were being hogged by the new guy. Later, I wondered what Laurence meant by "At least she tried." and concluded that he didn't deserve quite as much gratitude from me.

Friday 5th April

11pm

Went to Mam`s with fish and chips, they forgot the vinegar, so a very grumpy rant from her because her vinegar is not as good as chip shop vinegar! I offered to buy her some bottled chip shop vinegar next Friday in case they forgot again but she thinks I should just pay more attention when they are wrapping up the chips.

Saturday 6th April

Craft fair

Quiz night 8pm

QUIZ NIGHT

It`s Back!

The Quiz in the garden will resume on the 6^{th of} April

(First Saturday of the month from now until October)

Quiz Masters – Simon Williams and Merlin Jones

Teams of four (£4)

Refreshments available and Raffle

Starts promptly at 8pm

(If raining, go to big hall upstairs)

NB: IF YOUR TEAM IS LESS THAN 4 YOU STILL HAVE TO PAY £4!!!! REMEMBER PEOPLE, THIS IS FOR ALL THOSE LESS FORTUNATE THAN YOURSELVES!!!

11pm

Very quiet at craft fair, so much so that Si and I considered refunding the table fees, in the end we offered them a half price table for next time. As we sat together, eating lunch, Si said, "Why did we call it Weeble's?" I have no idea. One of us was probably drunk.

First quiz of the year was off to a good start! Except for a heated altercation with a man who says it is unfair he has to pay £4 for the quiz because he has come on his own, I suggested he could share a table with others who didn't have any friends either, he took this as an insult for some weird reason and demanded his money back before storming out and saying that I would be sorry! I was selling raffle tickets and Gwendolin was there with Merlin, her mother was babysitting, so she helped me. This is the first time she has been out without the kids since New Year. Always looking for a babysitter she said. You are so good with children, she said. I suddenly remembered it was time to check on the coffee urn in the kitchen and scurried away like the little rat I am.

I love kids but I`m *not* very good with them, they walk all over me, literally. Especially the little monsters at the "Small Minds" after school club.

Sunday 7th April

7pm

Richard and Mam are coming with me to next month`s "Quiz in the Garden" This is really nice of them because it means that I won`t have to either sit on my own, join up with strangers or mooch around looking useful trying to avoid getting accosted by mothers looking for babysitters. Going to get ready now for Singles Nite!

11pm

Glenda couldn't go to Singles Nite! She has a really bad cold, so I bravely went along anyway, I was very nervous and the people we sit with seemed incredibly scary now that I was alone. Don't get me wrong, they are very nice but I don`t understand their jokes and they can be very lewd! Worse than that is that I have made no effort at all to get to know them and I can`t even remember their names, gave up trying to fit in and sneaked home early. Why is it so hard to do small talk?

I Passed Derrick on the way out, securely embedded among Grumpy Lady's large noisy table of friends, I waved and said hello to him and received a baleful glare from Grumpy in return, bless! I think she will be wearing the trousers in that relationship, but he looks perfectly happy. It takes all sorts as Mam would say.

Tuesday 9th April

Take Mam out for lunch

11pm

Maggie Stamps has turned her little post office into a little coffee shop, so I took Mam there for lunch. Maggie seems ancient but is only in her sixties, Mam says it's too much sunbathing and being an older mother, apparently she was in her 40's when she gave birth to her one and only, and no sign of a father, says Mam.

In pride of place on one of the walls is a very large canvas of a woman and a baby posing in front of a beach. Slightly skewwhiff, so the subjects look as if they might slide into the sea,

"Ooh, that's lovely" says Mam

Maggie preens and simpers "My daughter Maureen with her new baby"

Then a really boring conversation ensued about how Maureen had moved away to England, met the love of her life, got married and bob`s your uncle, got pregnant! That`s the gist of it, it was a much longer conversation with Mam telling her that she couldn`t have any grandchildren because I had problems in that area.

The baby in the photo looked like all babies, no hair and fat, Maureen was skinny, and had a mouth like a prune. She was wearing a huge pair of sunglasses and a massive pink floppy hat.

I was scrutinising the canvas on the wall, wondering if I should try to straighten it up when I realised it was in Cornwall. "Oh, that`s St Michael`s Mount! Is that where your daughter has moved to? Is that your daughter? Do you remember Mam? Dai and I went there for our honeymoon! You booked us a week in that fisherman`s cottage, just outside Penzance."

Mam smiled fondly and was about to elaborate on my comment I expect, praising Cornwell and cream teas, but Maggie Stamps smile had turned downwards and she had whipped out her little order pad saying rudely that she couldn`t hang around gossiping all day with customers.

Mam is very pissed off at this abrupt change in Maggie's attitude and said she was not hungry after all and could we leave now please. So we had fish and chips in Luigi`s instead and Mam said she would tell all her friends about how Maggic Stamps was so rude that we had to walk out.

Good job for Maggie Stamps that Mam hasn't got any friends, they are either not speaking to her or they are dead.

Wednesday 10th April

11pm

When I was in Maggie`s café yesterday I noticed she had sellotaped a job advert to the mirror in the ladies toilet. She was looking for a part time assistant. Anyway I`m thinking, I could learn to cook there and get free food. Then when I`ve mastered the art of running a little café I could open my own,. I would have mismatched chairs and china and Laura Asley tablecloths, lush!

I popped in there on the way home from work, Maggie was clearing tables so I seized the opportunity to show her how willing I was and started piling mugs onto a waiting tray, but as soon as she saw me, she retreated behind her counter and shouted, "We're closed!"

I continued clearing the tables and with a lovely friendly smiley voice said "I've come about the job." Well! She rushed out from behind the counter and man-handled me out the door saying that there was no job for me and she knew what I was up to. I stood outside in shock to be honest, made worse by her saying, "stay out of my café Arwen Davies!" How does she know my name? I'm not that famous!

I know Mam was rude to her but no need for all that!

Saturday 13th April

11pm

Mam popped into the craft fair on her Zimmer frame to tell me she has booked us on Sensational Senior Holidays. Four bastard days in a mystery location, again. Four days of pushing her around in that bastard wheelchair, eating chopped to a pulp meat and three veg and tinned tomato soup in a faded Victorian hotel. Three bastard nights of cabaret with Uncle Phil (North Country Legend) the singer and jovial entertainment manager. I have gone right off these holidays especially since Dai used the one in 2017 to sneak Delyth into the marital bed (Bastard!) and she took the opportunity to persuade him to leave me shortly afterwards! (Marriage Wrecker!)

I offered Mam a lift home after the craft fair to save her getting a taxi, so she sat there in the café area passing the time by colouring in bookmarks and chatting to people. Sold a surprising number of commissions to naive people who think she is a sweet elderly lady helping her only childless widowed depressed daughter out. Loads of customers pressed their £3 into my hands and filed their drawings in the bespoke bookmarks tray saying things like "I hope life looks up for you cariad" So Mam can come again, I`m not proud!

Sunday 14th April *Palm Sunday-Sul y Blodau*

12.30am

How long have I been coming to singles night now? I still haven't found anyone I like, Glenda thinks I`m a bit too picky and obsessed with good looking men, she has a theory that the good looking ones are bastards, so it's best to go for the ugly ones, but I can't go along with that! Good job I love dancing and the music. Glenda has been making a bit of a play for Derrick but he only has eyes for Grumpy Woman now, which is a shame really because he and Glenda would make a lovely couple, she not so subtly ambushes him when he goes to the bar, she really should give up, he is smitten.

DJ has lost his Meatloaf music, says he will have a good look for it, but he is not hopeful, he thinks it fell out of his car on the way home from a gig.

Thursday 18th April

11pm

We were all standing in the community garden today because one of the Bingo Sessions women has died and the centre was part of her last journey, all her mates were there in a little huddle holding up a home-made banner which said.

"Full house at last Maisie. RIP the Bingo Bunch"

Anyway, I was totally shocked and very pleasantly surprised to see that Dai the Death was driving the hearse! He gave me a quick wave as he passed by, I smiled and waved back, earning dismayed noises and annoyed tuts from the grief-stricken bingo bunch. He looked very lovely in his funeral get-up. He has obviously taken over the business, either that or he helps out with the driving.

Friday 19th April *Good Friday*

11pm

Told Mam about Maisie from the bingo bunch funeral passing by, she went very quiet and said Maisie is younger than her and that it`s a bit of a worry, in an effort to lighten the atmosphere, I said she had better get on with the death cleaning then, she replied that I was a very cold uncaring person and no wonder I didn't have a boyfriend. What the fuck?

Saturday 20th April

11pm

Really busy at the craft fair, but I didn`t sell a lot of bookmarks. Kelvin who sells sweets and rock had got a load of plastic eggs from the wholesaler and had filled them up with mini eggs, I bought one for Owen. I asked him if he had washed his hands properly before he filled the eggs, he told me to F Off. Charming!

I`m worried now that if I give the mini eggs to Owen and Kelvin didn`t wash his hands, that Owen will come down with a disease and it will be my fault. I asked Mam for advice, she said, "Boys are immune to germs." Are they?

Sunday 21st April *Easter Sunday*

7pm

Got up early to take Mam to chapel. I walked up to her door to get her and help her into the car, she was waiting for me with a carrier bag. "Happy Easter," she said, I gave her a kiss on the cheek, and opened the bag, "Oh thanks Mam, it`s a cake pretending to be an Easter egg! How clever, shall we take it to Rhiannon's?"

"No need, I've made another one!" I have to admit, she seems much happier since she has been coming to lunch every Sunday, as I was musing about this, she whacked me with the end of her stick "Hurry up, you are making me late!" I gave her a lecture about using violence against your children.

Owen was overloaded with chocolate eggs, I suggested he donate some to the food bank, Albie said I was obsessed with the food bank and was always going through his cupboards and stealing his food, that`s a lie! I once took four cans of beans from his place that were close to the use by date! Conversation then took off about food banks and the request for surplus eggs got lost in the argument that followed. As I was leaving, Owen gave me £2 out of his pocket money for the food bank and said, "You can buy something healthy for them instead Auntie Arwen". What a sweetheart!

1pm

I thought I would make a bit more of an effort tonight at the dance, so smiled a bit more and wore my new sparkly silver top with black trousers. It sort of worked, I got more dances.

I was dancing a slow dance with one of the men from out of town and he asked me what I liked doing, I said I liked reading and that at the moment I was re-reading Gormenghast. He was very quiet so I carried on talking and told him that I really loved the DVD as well but for different reasons.

Well! He stopped dancing, held me away from him, looked at me with a very perplexed expression and said. "Are you for fucking real?" so I left him there alone on the dancefloor and went back to my seat. Bastard!

Oh Yeah! This thing about men not talking to one another is rubbish because later when I went out for a fag, Smelly Dennis smirked at me, nudged his friend Aneuryn from Kier Hardy Retirement Apartments by the harbour and said, hardly able to stop sniggering, "Read any good books lately Arwen?"

DJ has lost his Dire Straits music as well as Meatloaf now, I expect Rod Stewart will be the next to go, DJ isn't very good in my opinion.

Monday 22nd – 28th April

Started asking around about Dai.

Monday

Long conversation about Dai's disappearance with Si which then degenerated into the fucking fantasy realm.

Tuesday

Spoke to Les in the Spar, he was a bit shocked to see me because the boy who works on the till went to look for him and told him that a really posh little angry woman wanted to see him! Really! I am neither posh nor angry! As luck would have it, Delyth was hanging around outside the Spar hoping to bump into Les on his fag break, so spoke to her as well.

Called into the taxi office to speak to Terry, the driver we always used. Had to listen to a long rant about how when he was on his minibreak in London, his so called friend and fellow taxi driver, Barrie Spink, used Terry`s absence to offer cut price travel to Terry`s disloyal regulars and now they have all switched allegiance to Bastard Barrie.

Wednesday

Popped into Albie`s to ask him if he had any ideas about Dai`s disappearance, he and Ken were poring over a tourist map of Cornwell but folded it up when I had a look at it and pointed out Penzance where I had honeymooned with Dai.

Thursday

Went around to the workshop to speak to Badger, we had a chat about Dai and then about me needing new bookshelves, so he is popping around to give me a quote. Badger also kindly phoned Steve the workshop owner for me, although he had nothing to add that was new.

Friday

Asked Mam. Then spent an hour listening to how she warned me not to marry him (She didn`t) and where was the slice of lemon for her fish gone? We couldn`t find it anywhere, so we might have to change chip shops, she says, unless I can be more alert. She will have forgotten by next week.

Sunday

Questioned Richard and Rhiannon and then lost really badly at Monopoly because my mind is so full of my investigations about Dai`s disappearance! Tamping! To compensate, Rhiannon gave me the leftovers, even though it was their turn for fry-ups.

Monday 29th April

11pm

I`ve had an exhausting week gathering the information from people who might have an insight into Dai`s death/disappearance, but it`s done now. Here are the results.

Me-I think he has run off to a more exciting life, somewhere by the sea with a beachside café and surf shop, a bit like Summer Bay, he has probably bleached his hair and is wearing loud shirts and drinking lager out of bottles, he is a carpenter, so will always find work, building bespoke kitchens or converting garages into games rooms.

Si-Fell off the headland into a wormhole and is now a sex slave on a planet full of very strong women.

Delyth-Let it go Arwen, he is with God now, singing hymns and at peace (I had no idea she was religious, she sounded like my Mam!)

Les-I don`t know Arwen, I hope he doesn't turn up again, sorry mind.

Rhiannon-Maybe he was depressed, I want to believe he is alive somewhere and I hope he is but he would have found a way to tell us he is ok…wouldn`t he?

Richard-Between you and me Arwen, I think he has just run away from his responsibilities and is sunning himself somewhere, if he ever turns up here, I will give him a piece of my mind for putting Rhiannon through this.

Badger-"I think he is dead, he was very depressed about his love life, said it was all a complete mess and wanted a way out."

Uncle Albie-Dead.

Taxi driver-The week Dai disappeared he was on a mini break in London. He was sure about this because when they got back, it was Badger who turned up at their house to finish off the shelves in the dining room and he had told him about Dai jumping off the Head.

Workshop owner-Steve last saw him when he paid the rent at the end of January, 6 months in advance, he told him to send the receipt to Badger. He has no idea if Dai is alive or dead.

Mam-Dead, otherwise he would have turned up by now, like a bad penny.

Of the people I asked (including me) four think he's dead, four are either undecided or don't know and three think he is alive. Carry on with the investigations, I think.

May

the force be with you

<u>*Intentions*</u>

Be nicer

Be more interesting

Find a new job

Get a boyfriend

Find a new hobby

Be a better daughter

Be a better auntie

Write longer poems

Find out what really happened to Dai.

Nothing to cross off again! So disappointing.

Wednesday 1st May

11pm

Even though I have stopped routinely checking up on Albie and Ken, I popped in there after work with some jam doughnuts. They are doing fine, Ken has made the spare bedroom his own and has bought himself a glass cabinet thing to store his boxing trophies in, he is a bit of a dark horse, is Ken. Although that explains his broken nose and cauliflower ears, love him.

I went to Poetry Group, I like short poems but I don't think I'm very good at Haikus, just can't get the lines right! My versions seem ok to me, but when I said this to the others they sarcastically ganged up on me and referred to the fact that the Japanese have been perfecting the haiku for hundreds of years. There is nothing worse than a room full of bitter sarcastic poets.

My death is nothing

More than a crow black fluttering

Of aged rags

I changed it quickly to this and read it out to them again.

My death is nothing

More than a crow black ~~Fluttering~~ Fluttring

Of aged ~~rags~~ rag-gehz

It didn't help, they still hated it.

Saturday 4th May

11pm

Today was the fourth of May, Si was in his element and kept saying, "May the fourth be with you," he had turned up looking like an overweight hairy Hans Solo, the crafters loved it, fair play. One of the many reasons I love Saturday Craft Fairs is that even if you don't sell much, you meet such interesting people. My free table is permanently by the coffee area now because I laminated a sign and taped it to the wall behind, "Reserved for community centre staff," and opposite me this week was Trudy the clairvoyant. She kept beckoning to me and in the end I sauntered over to her table.

"Hiya, you ok?"

"I have news for you from the other side" she whispers.

"Oh aye" I whisper back. (Mustn't upset the fee payers)

Trudy clutches at my arm, "From a loved one on the other side."

I am shocked, "Who?"

Turns out she doesn't know who it is, news from the other side is usually vague and seen through a glass darkly, according to Trudy (What the fuck!). She nagged me to choose four cards from an ancient Tarot Pack, so I picked the nine of pentacles, the fool, the tower and the ten of cups. All about opportunities and new beginnings, said Trudy. Then she produced another pack of cards, and said, go on, pick one for clarification, she fans out the cards, and I pick out St Michael the archangel. He is being very manly with a sword on top of a castle by the sea. She waved her hand to a chair placed on the end of the table and said, "Sit there Arwen, and I'll read the cards for you." I was desperate to get away and luckily a string of customers turned up, so I could retreat to my table. Later as I was packing up, Trudy came over with a list of the cards I had chosen "Keep these safe and I`ll read them for you another time."

Keep these safe

Nine of pentacles

The fool

The tower

Ten of cups

Michael the archangel

I thought I was very kind listening to her ramblings, love her. I said "Thank you so much Trudy" and gave her a bookmark. "Be Kind" one of my best sellers.

Managed to get a team together for the quiz. Because today is the 4th of May, all the quiz questions are about Star Wars, I did guess that this would be the case, so swotted up on it last night and would have won if Si`s friends from the "Star Wars appreciation Society (Cerrig-Mor Chapter)" hadn't turned up and swept the board, spectacularly.

I did come second though, even though my team was made up of Richard, who always mixes Star Wars up with Star Trek, Pat Potatoes the gardener who is a nice man but who's specialist subject is vegetables, obviously, and my mother who just got out her neon orange crocheting and said I'm only here to make up the numbers. Si mentioned to the Cerrig-Mor Star Wars obsessives that I made bespoke bookmarks. So! I have a huge order of fifty bookmarks for their branch of the appreciation society. They handed me a rough drawing of Yoda with his light sabre, issuing a stern command "Cerrig Mor Star Wars Chapter meets every Monday! Be there you will!"

Sunday 5th May

7pm

Remembered to return Rhiannon's smart black dress today, but she said I could keep it, not only that but after lunch, we had a lovely time going through her wardrobe, looking for other dresses that were too small for her. I found a lovely burgundy one. I'll wear it tonight with my new shoes.

Singles night is going well, I now have two suitable dresses to alternate with the very sparkly top and black trousers, the DJ still can't find Meat Loaf though.

My new dancing shoes squeak, which is quite satisfying I think, but Glenda finds it annoying and said they are not even dancing shoes but just old lady silver sandals and do nothing for me. I told her that I prefer comfort over fashion, especially when it comes to dancing and also they are a step up from my black court shoes, bought in 2009 especially for funerals. By 11 o clock most of the women on our table are complaining about their feet but, thanks to my comfy dancing shoes, my feet are fine!

Still haven't seen anyone I would consider going out with, although there was one man who I thought might be ok, until I overheard him describing one of the women on the dancefloor in a very derogatory and misogynistic way, when I complained to Sanjeev and Sharon, they brushed it off as high spirits and the drink. Sandra said if they banned all the people who weren't politically correct, it would be more of a very small gathering than a dance, and that they would only need a couple of tables at most.

Friday 10th May

11pm

Went to Mam's as usual, for fish and chips, and she has informed me, that on Monday after I have been to work, we are going through her funeral plans! I say, "What has brought this about?" It turns out that she has read about a terrible coach accident in the Alps where an old woman was tragically killed. My argument that a mystery trip to Torquay in Devon probably, (I'm going by past mystery trip experiences) is not exactly going to lead to a catastrophic plummet off an Alp is dismissed, she is not having any of it. My only consolation is that she is using Dai the Death's company and finger's crossed, it is him who is coming to arrange her funeral, I casually asked her if she knew who would be doing it, pretending that I knew one of the office staff, and she said it was Mr Jones himself. I hope it's not his father.

Sunday 12th May

1am

Mam was in her element at Rhiannon's, proudly announcing our up-coming appointment with Caradoc

Jones & Jones the undertakers, asking for advice about funeral songs. This degenerated into a raucous sing-song, and finally ended when Owen did his impression of Wham and sang "Wake me up before you go go."

DJ still can`t find his Meatloaf music, so annoying. I have offered to take in my CD`s for him, but he said he doesn't think that would work, a bit defeatist if you ask me.

13th Monday

Make a list for Si re important stuff to do while I`m away

Pack

Go around Mam`s for funeral plans.

11pm

Went to Mam`s to go through her funeral plans. I was conflicted because I wanted to see Dai again (fingers crossed it was him and not his Dad) and find out more about him and nervous because if it was him, that I would be my usual say it first, think about it afterwards self.

I also seem to have a knack of upsetting him for some reason that I cannot fathom. Was it ok to wear my best clothes and put a bit of make up on? I was much too excited at the thought of meeting Dai again, to hide this, I smirked at Mam and said, "Well, off on the hols tomorrow Mam, I have to say mind that most people want advice on how many pair of knickers they should pack or how to get their suitcase down from the attic, you are the only person I know who wants advice on whether the coffin should be oak or beech."

"That's enough of that!" she said, "You are so nasty and sarcastic these days, I worry for you." She has no idea of the difference between jovial wit and sarcastic nastiness.

It was Dai who turned up, I let him in, we made eye contact as I took his coat off him, saying "It's very warm in here!" and I swear he was blushing as much as I was. I thought middle aged people were too old to blush.

Turns out I was doing my funeral plans as well, he was quite insistent about that, much to Mam's surprise as well as my own. so here are the results in a handy A4 ring binder, supplied free by Dai.

Your Death

Made Easy

NAME

ADDRESS

NEXT OF KIN

MARITAL STATUS

(Name, address and next of kin all seemed like appropriate questions, but I thought marital status was a bit strange, especially when after I said separated, possibly widowed, his next questions were "Not going out with anyone then" and "Are you likely to be in the

*near future?" Weird but triggering hopeful sensations
in my heart area for some reason.)*

TYPE OF COFFIN

Barbara – Beech

Arwen – cardboard

FLOWERS

Barbara – Anything but Lilies

Arwen – Lilies

MUSIC

Barbara –

Robbie Williams, Angels/The old rugged cross/The
Lord is my Shepherd/I did it my way/Time to say
goodbye (Welshman with the nice voice)

Arwen–

Meatloaf/Dire Straits/Killers/Queen/ Adele/ Tracy
Chapman/ West Life/Scissor Sisters. (Will add more
later)

EULOGY

Barbara – Rev John (The God) from the Baptist Chapel.

Arwen – 3 minutes silence.

PLACE

Barbara – Baptist chapel, burial.

Arwen – Cremation at the crem.

SPECIAL REQUESTS

Barbara – everyone in black with a bit of purple.

Arwen – no

THE WAKE (Buffet prices supplied on request at time of death)

Barbara – the church hall

Arwen – any pub she is not banned from

It took ages, and a lot of my answers were flippant and thoughtless for such a serious topic, but to be fair, it was a bit of a spontaneous exercise for me. Dai said he is used to the form filling taking a long time and that he found my sense of humour refreshing. He is still very nice, we talked a bit about school and our jobs. He is the sort of man I should be dating, kind, clean, philosophical, intelligent and with that slightly dejected air that I find so attractive and which must be quite an asset in his line of work.

As I was showing him out, he said "You know my name`s not Dai, don`t you?"

"Haha" I laughed, covertly scanning the receipt for the down payment "Of course! It`s Caradoc isn't it!"

He gave me a withering look, "That`s my dad`s name!" he said grumpily and refused my offer to hold his bag while he struggled into his coat. He still gave me his business card though and said I could phone him any time I wanted if I have any questions about my requests, "Or if," he inclined his head towards Mam "you know, you need me?"

Caradoc Jones &Jones

Independent Funeral Directors

Looking after your dearly departed

Since 1929

On a mission now to find out his name. I took a photo of his business card before I put in my purse just in case I lost it. Kept remembering how kind and shy he was in Geography A level, and how he admired my drawings of various fault lines, and my map of Cerrig-Mor.

I asked Mam what her problem was with lilies, she said the pollen got everywhere and stained your clothes and they reminded her of death!

May 14th Tuesday

11pm in Cornwall

Brought my journal with me, going to write up the day`s events every night as usual. Terry the Taxi dropped us off at 7am outside the Co-op, the coach driver is having a fag behind the bus, so I join him. "Smoker are you love," he says, "Yeah" I say, "Any smoking stops on the way Drive?" He promises to do his best and that if I want to help I can fake the need to go to the toilet when I see any services coming up, so I have to make sure I sit in the window seat on the left hand side. I say, what if I really want to go to the toilet and you think it`s just an excuse for a fag but you're not in the mood for one? He thought about this and said, "If you really need the toilet just say your desperate otherwise just say can we stop for the toilets. Come on then, let's get this show on the road." As he swung my little suitcase into the hold thing he said "Bloody hell! What have you got in here, bricks?" Maybe I went a bit mad with the books. I just laughed and hurried to get on the bus, forcing Mam to move so that I could sit in the window seat, left hand side.

Eventually, we were off, I really annoy Mam by occasionally saying, "Are we there yet?" She has no sense of humour at all. On the way we picked up more people, most of them are elderly, any who aren't elderly get Mam`s full attention, "Ooh, he looks nice, about your age, probably her son, he reminds me of the bank manager, might be good marriage material Arwen!" in a very loud voice that would remind any Pride and Prejudice fans of Mrs fucking Bennet! Then, "Ooh look at her, and look at her daughter"! Sometimes she talks much too loudly in my opinion so when she says "Oh bless! Down`s Syndrome!, her poor mother!" I said "Mam for God's sake, shut up!" The mother and daughter seemed to be having a mild tussle about who sat in the window seat, so I hoped they hadn`t heard Mam`s insensitive remarks, the young woman won the fight and settled into the window seat and we were off again.

I leant over and whispered in Mam`s ear, "I expect when we got on the bus, everyone looked at us and thought `look at that bossy old woman in the horrible jacket and her downtrodden carer` that`s what everyone thinks when they see us, that I`m your downtrodden carer and thank God they are not wearing your jacket." I spent the rest of the journey feeling guilty for being so horrible to her. She gave me the silent treatment for a while and refused to hand me the tuna sandwiches and orange juice.

I was desperate for a fag after this bout of daughterly vitriol, but too nervous to pull the toilet scam, but lo and behold, we stopped anyway at the Magor Services. Drive, whose name is Alun, said next break is in England, so stock up on snacks and things. Why? Are English snacks less snackey or something?

I dashed off the bus and stood outside having a quick fag while Mam slowly moved along the aisle, glaring at me at every opportunity. By the time Mam was off the bus, I had her lightweight wheelchair up and ready for her queenship to sit down in. I pushed her to the toilets and then the café area. Once she was settled down with a Welsh cake and a decaff coffee I headed outside for another rollup. There were about six smokers including Alun sitting at one of the wooden tables, desperately smoking. He shuffled up and I perched on the end of the bench trying not to touch him. I said "Hiya" and the young woman with Down`s said, "I heard what your mother said, so bastard rude."

"I am so sorry" I said, she smiled, so encouraged by this, I smiled back and said, "How can I make up for her bastard rudeness?" They all had a few suggestions mainly unprintable, which Drive put a stop to by declaring that she was my mother for God`s sake, but all's well that ends well and now me and Jessica are friends and smoking buddies. She confided in me that her mother is much worse than mine, and that I should think myself lucky.

Arrived at the mystery destination, it`s Marazion, near Penzance, what a coincidence! The hotel is large and purple from the outside. As we were waiting for Alun to get our stuff out of the boot, Mam gave a little gasp and started pointing to the beach, which was across the road from our hotel. To cut a long story short, she is convinced she saw Dai on the beach with some tall thin woman and a baby, I saw no one who looked like Dai, just a busload of hen party girls in garish straw hats and pink tee-shirts milling around taking photos of each other and swigging lager from cans. Anyway, she was so convinced that it was Dai that we had to go and buy her a pair of binoculars to scan the beach with. I'll be a prisoner in this 1980`s throwback of a hotel now, with her sitting obsessively in the sunlounge bay window, eyes glued on the beach, demanding tea from the hospitality tray. We went off to the shops after ham and cheese sandwiches and chips on the side to buy the binoculars, I suggested an eye patch and a telescope seeing as we are in pirate county, she looked at me with that look she has and said "I should have known you would be stupid about it". I will offer to buy them off her once we get home so that I can do a bit of beach scanning of my own.

Mam settled in for beach watch, I settled in for a lush break with books, snacks, non-alcoholic lager, and occasional trips to the smoking shelter. All us smokers have set up a group chat and we try co-ordinate our trips to the shelter, although some of them smoke too much in my opinion. At 8pm we assembled in the lounge bar to listen to the resident crooner. Why do old people like those terrible songs from the sixties?

Wednesday 15th May

11pm

Today's trip was either a visit to the nearby gardens or lunch at St Michael's Mount bar and café, Alun was clearly more enthusiastic about the Mount and warned us of the steep paths at the gardens, he told us this (uncorroborated) tale of an accident that happened last year when a poor old dear careered down the path to the cliff edge after her carer forgot to put her wheelchair brakes on, he was looking sympathetically at Mam when he said this, because she was the one who made "How lovely" and "I love a garden" noises when he was giving us the itinerary for the day. So all the old people chose the Mount, even though it took ages for everyone to get there on the little boats.

Went to a pub on the seafront this evening, while Mam and the other old people rushed to the lounge bar to listen to "Kevin the Crooner" (requests accepted) and sat watching as people walked over to St Michaels Mount on the causeway. I had this niggling feeling that I have been here recently but I haven't, the only time I have been here was on our honeymoon. Then later, with Mam tucked up in bed catching up on the soaps it dawned on me, the pub is the same one where Maggie Stamp`s daughter must have had her photo taken so Mam might have seen *her* on the beach with her baby and her new husband. Mam`s eyesight isn`t great, she is very short sighted, in fact, she should view the world through a pair of binoculars permanently! I woke her up to ask her, and she agreed that the man might have just looked like Dai, but she was not convinced at all.

I love our smoking group. There's me, Alun the driver, Meena- a beautician, Jessica- works in Asda, Harry – lives in his bedroom at his mother's house and works for a tech company and Gordon, who is very old, and doesn't have a phone, so Harry gives him a knock on the way down to the shelter. Meena has this theory that banning indoors smoking means that smokers have become more sociable than non-smokers and that we should cherish this fact and remember it when our family constantly go on at us to give it up. Hmm, interesting, needs more investigation. But to be fair, we smokers always had have ice breakers on the tips of our tongues, my favourite is, "Oh hell! Forgotten my lighter" which without fail kick starts a conversation and the whipping out of lighters from stranger's pockets.

Thursday 16th May

11pm in Cornwall

Mam has given up on beach watch so we went out for lunch and to buy souvenirs and postcards. We had to make another trip later to post them, it`s alright for her, she is not pushing herself in that bastard wheelchair! As I pushed her about, She said "You know I never wanted children, when I had you my life was ruined, but when all is said and done, I`m glad I`ve got you, you do your best, don`t you." Well, I was so happy at this revelation that I bought her a blue lapis lazuli brooch shaped like forget me not flower, from the "Wings of an Angel" esoteric gifts shop. I`ll give it to her on the way home.

I also bought some tarot cards and a book on how to read them. Mam asked if I was considering a new career as a witch, I said why not, perhaps I can buy a spell book next and turn you into an old toad. That`s a lie, I didn`t say that at all, I just laughed at her quip and said, "Come on, I`ll give you a reading Mam!" she crossed herself and said The Lord would be wondering how she managed to produce such a devil worshipping heathen.

When she says things like this it's easy to assume she is kidding, but the truth is, she is deadly serious. I searched through the pack and found the cards I drew at the Craft Fair, laid them out on the bed and found the meanings from the "How to read the Tarot" book.

Nine of pentacles - *prosperity, wealth, security (Bring it on!)*

The fool – *new beginning, opportunity and potential (New job?)*

The tower – *allows you to tear down and start again in a direction you would previously never dared to consider (Definitely a new job!)*

The lovers – *this card is all about choice, and summons up idealised visions of love, often based on infatuations and lust (New boyfriend? Dai the Death?)*

The other card was an Angel card, Michael the Archangel, googled him, he is a very powerful angel and uses his sword to protect people. I could do with a bit of protecting, to be fair, anyone could, couldn't they. Anyway it's a good card, I'm beginning to sound like Trudy. I don't really believe in all this airy fairy stuff but

I have to admit I am feeling very uplifted by the meanings of the cards I chose. Seems like 2019 might be a very good year for me! I need to get on with searching for a new job and finding out Dai the Death`s real name so that he can stop being annoyed with me.

Mam couldn`t find her binoculars, so after much fussing and emptying of bags and drawers I went down to the lounge to see if she had left them there. She had, I stood looking out of the window, the lights of the town reflected in the water were mesmerising. I decided that there is no harm in adding the fact that Mam is convinced she saw Dai yesterday to the list I have compiled, because if he has disappeared and is not dead, he must be somewhere and Cornwall is as good a place as anywhere.

Dai`s Disappearance amended list

1. *Dai disappeared on 3rd February at about 11pm.*

   No body.

2. *Sold important and treasured possessions prior to disappearing.*

3. *Left his van outside Delyth's bungalow with the keys in it.*

4. *Left three notes. (to me, to Delyth and one by the standing stones)*

5. *Police not bothered.*

6. *Never used the word suicide or death in the notes.*

7. *Mam thought she saw him in Marazion.*

Friday 17th May

Pack

Go home

Ask Terry Taxi to make a detour to the chip shop

11pm

Home at last! I`m going to really miss my smoking friends, there were lots of cwtches and a bit of a plan to meet up at Christmas in Cardiff. Even as we made these plans we all knew they probably wouldn't happen but at least we have the What's-app group. I hope we do keep in touch I am really really fond of them.

Messaged Dianne earlier to tell her we are home and mentioned that Mam said she was glad she had me.

I said maybe she has a hidden disability that makes her occasionally rude and cold, and maybe I should take this into account and it would explain the fact that she didn't like me touching her or never cwtched me when I was growing up. Dianne added a shocked emoji to my message phoned me immediately saying, "You want her to have a hidden disability because *you* have one and then you would have found something in common to bond over and you could forgive her for her atrocious behaviour, don't be late with the activities list for the June newsletter and try typing it up this time, your handwriting is practically illegible Arwen!"

A few things here-

> *1.She is really bossy and outspoken since she started the menopause*
>
> *2. Do I behave atrociously? Do I have a hidden disability?*
>
> *3. My handwriting is perfectly legible, so no need to type it up!*

Saturday 18th May

11pm

Si loved his clotted cream fudge and his "Penzance Pirate" bandana and terrorised all the old ladies at the craft fair by jumping out in front of them and shouting, "Ooh Arr!." He said he lost the list I gave him and just spent the whole week enjoying himself instead.

Sunday 19th May

7pm

Asked Rhiannon if she knew Dai the Death's real name and if she thought I had a hidden disability, she looked perplexed, and said she didn't know his name and she thought I probably had Asperger's or something. I'm really shocked that she doesn't know Dai the Death's real name, because usually she knows everything. Can you find out for me I said. Ok she said, come on Arwen, mash the potatoes mun, they are going cold.

So, the temperature of potatoes is more important than my love life!

11pm

This evening at Singles Nite! I thought I saw Dai the Death hovering by the door, looking lovely in his funeral suit. I sauntered nonchalantly over, rehearsing what to say, but when I got there, either it wasn't him or he had gone. I asked Sandra and Sanjeev who were sitting at their table, adding up the entrance money if they had seen a very good looking man who looked a bit like Ross Poldark with short hair, but they hadn`t, as I was walking dejectedly back to our table, Sandra said, "Who is this Ross then love? Has he been here before?" I wish!

Monday 20th May

Asked Si what Dai the Death`s real name was, "Dai innit?" he said, Typical! Shouldn`t have asked him because then we had to have a stupid conversation about why I wanted to know and with Si concluding that I fancied Dai to death. Very bloody funny.

Saturday 25th May

11pm

Had a nice look around at the other tables at the craft fair, took some photos of the merchandise to pin up in the foyer, and reluctantly bought a pound shop book off Nigel Next Table for £2 for writing my poetry in, it`s quite an improvement on scrap paper. Maybe it will help me to write longer poems!

Sunday 26th May

11pm

Same old Sunday routine, good job I love food, family and dancing.

Still no sign of Meatloaf or Dire Straits.

Tuesday 28th May

Mam gave me a thankyou present for going to Cornwall with her. A very expensive gift voucher (Hmm!).

Angel Starfire 028

Certified Beauty Consultant

Come and relax at my fully refurbished studios and let me transform your life with advice and a facial massage

(Bring your favourite clothes and your make-up bag)

Complimentary tea and coffee provided

No 2 the stable blocks, Ty Mawr

Two hours at the beauty spa in Ty Mawr`s converted stable block discussing my lack of dress sense and the disgusting contents of my make up bag. "Angel Starfire – Certified Beauty Consultant" turned out to be Ruth Morris from "The Banks" up by the caravan park. I didn't ask her outright if she remembered how her famous Chinese burns used to leave me crying in the toilets in year seven, and how guilty and relieved I felt when she found someone else to bully, because she had obviously received her Lifetime Amnesia Certificate, promptly awarded to all bullies on the day they leave school.

"Oh, hiya Arwen" she said, "I haven't seen you for ages love!" I put my seething resentment and thoughts of revenge aside and engaged in stupid conversations about my love of black, the unhealthy state of my make-up and Dai.

I find out that Dai, the bastard, came onto her once in the Green Man while he was with Delyth and that later that same evening she found Delyth in the toilets weeping because Dai was flirting "Outrageously!!" in the smoking shed with that tall blonde girl, who always wears designer clothes, even in the Co-op.

"What tall blonde girl?" I asked. Ruth binned my favourite eye-shadow and the eyebrow tweezers I got from a Christmas cracker.

"You know! That blonde girl, tall and skinny, big sticky out ears. How old is this mascara Arwen? I hope you don`t wear it! It`s a health disaster waiting to happen!"

I asked her if she knew Dai the Death`s real name and she said she went out with him a couple of times after school but they had nothing in common and that his real name was Gareth and that he was still single as far as she knew. She thinks his singleness is because of all those dead people in the back of his house, bit of a pong she said, really? Still hasn`t put me off mind, you can get used to anything, Si and Uncle Albie don`t exactly smell of roses.

So now I have his real name, his work`s phone number and his relationship status, it`s time to change my funeral plans.

My face is still red and blotchy, I don`t think I am made for face massages, but at least it didn`t hurt as much as the Chinese burns.

Friday 31st May

11pm

Glynys wants me to go to the school reunion for her year. Class of 1964 for fucks sake! They will all be around 70 years old! She`s begging me, harassing me actually, I said yes but she owes me for this one, its upstairs in the Green Man on the 19thJuly. I told her there were loads of stairs and no lift and she should consider her poor heart, which upset her for some reason. I am so annoyed, I only know Glynys because she runs the craft fair coffee shop, and even though she thinks she is my friend, she is not! Told Mam about it and she said I should see it as an opportunity and that if I make a bit of effort, I might meet someone! They will all be old enough to be my father for God`s sake!

June

Dare to dream

Intentions

Be nicer

Be more interesting

Find a new job

Get a boyfriend

Find a new hobby

Be a better daughter

Be a better auntie

Write longer poems

Find out what really happened to Dai.

Another month gone, no more of my intentions realised.

Saturday 1st June

6pm

Craft fair was quiet so I spent the whole time thinking about my funeral, thanks to you Mam! When George next door but one died, even though he was very old, loads of people came to his funeral. No one is going to come to mine because,

> a) I will be old hopefully so even my mother will be dead.

> b) I will be even grumpier than I am now.

I'll make an appointment with Gareth to change my funeral plan. Things I can change are:

Music select sadder songs maybe.

Choice of flowers wildflowers if possible?

Eulogy something clever and sad that will impress him, or ask him for *his* suggestions, men like you to ask their advice, in my opinion. Perhaps I could show him my poems and let him choose one. I'll have a look though my poems tomorrow and see if there is a good one. Off to the quiz now.

11pm

The man who shouted at me about having to pay £4 for his table, even though it was just him on his own, came to the quiz and triumphantly introduced me to his three friends. What a depressing day this has turned out to be.

Sunday 2nd June

1am

I am never going to meet anyone suitable at Singles Nite! Good job I like dancing, even though the music is terrible now that the DJ has refused to take anymore requests, Glenda says I have spoiled it for everyone, how come it's always my fault?

June 4th Tuesday

11pm

National cheese day, I love cheese, one of my favourites is that tube thing of cheese and ham, lush, although cheese purists would be sniffy about it I suppose. Cheese and ham tube spread is lovely with a slice of smoked ham in a sandwich, with cheese and onion crisps on the side and a rhubarb yoghurt for afters. I'm hungry now, just thinking about it. Also quite happy, cheese always makes me happy!

Does cheese really give you nightmares? I am having a lot of bad dreams about Dai and if cheese is the culprit I am going to have to cut down on it, I have eaten quite a lot of cheese today obviously, so if I have a nightmare tonight, I have only myself to blame.

Wednesday 5th June

11pm

Went to Poetry, had one more go at a haiku, got it right at last! Suck it up fellow poets!

Death, silent, brooding

Creeps to her bed at midnight

Gathers up her soul

Might use this haiku for my funeral, I'll show it to Gareth. I could get one of the poetry group to read it, if any of them are still alive and can be bothered to attend. It would be great coming from a poet; they will know how to read it properly. Lots of long pauses and all that malarky. I'll have to change it to past tense.

Thursday 6th June

1pm

Si said that Golden Pastures, the old peoples home by the Rusty Anchor are looking for cleaners, so I'm popping in there on the way home.

11pm

Popped into Golden pastures, the woman on reception gave me an application form and said I could have a job trial to see how I got on. Brilliant! I told her next Tuesday would be good for me, so I'm going in for 10am and shadowing an experienced worker. I could learn how to clean professionally and start my own business, I've got a hoover and one of those apron things with big pockets, it would be great.

Friday 7th June

11pm

Chip shop tonight as usual for mine and Mam`s dinner, I`m sitting there waiting for my fish and chips, staring at a home-made poster for the local food bank and feeling guilty for not having beans on toast and donating the money for my fish and chips to hungry people in need when Pop Jenkins leered at me and said "Cheer up Love, you look like you've been slapped by a rotting haddock!" He had no right to say that to me! If we are going to trade insults, I could comment on the fact that he has a beer gut so large he looks like he is having triplets! On the other hand, my resting feeling guilty face does look as if the world is about to end so instead I just smiled at him and said under my breath, "Fuck off fatman" except it wasn't under my breath, so I had 5 minutes of me refusing to repeat what I`d said and Pop breathing beer fumes all over me.

In the end I was rescued by Jackie shouting "Sixty five!" I excused myself from Pop`s questioning, picked up my fish and chips and scooted.

Told Mam what Pop Jenkin's said and she said miserable looking women trigger him because his ex-wife Elsie did actually look as if she might have been slapped by a rotting haddock and that was on a good day. She also said the reason he is always drunk is that Elsie ran away with his brother Elwyn, to Skegness to open a bed and breakfast, stealing his black Norton 750 first and swapping it for a badly sprayed orange escort van from Gilfach Goch. She is a font of local knowledge, is Mam.

Monday 10th June

5pm

Finally got around to contacting Gareth about my funeral plan changes. I texted him this morning, because I was too embarrassed about not remembering his name to phone him, I said...

Hiya Gareth,

It's Arwen, we went through my funeral plans the other week and you said I could change some of the details, so if you wouldn't mind calling me to arrange a meeting, that would be great x

He called me back almost immediately! He is coming round this evening at six to discuss the changes, I asked Geoff if I could go home early to tidy up a bit, he said, why not, you do nothing anyway, how rude! Bought real coffee and homemade cake from the deli on the way. Because I wanted to make an effort, I tried out the new makeup that Ruth Morris forced me to buy, but I looked like a clown, so I`ve washed it off, I don`t think Bleu Azure eyeshadow is for me, or Cream with Peaches lipstick. I am so glad I asked him, thing is, shall I put music on? While I wait? Decided to play my Tracey Chapman cd, which is suitable for arranging funerals in my opinion, subdued and soulful.

11pm

Rearrangements for funeral went well, he had changed out of his black work clothes and brought a bottle of chilled prosecco with him, I put the cake into the cupboard and said wow, that would go really well with a tuna pasta salad! He was very impressed at how I threw it together from store cupboard ingredients and a frozen garlic baguette. It turns out that he still likes me as much as I like him and as we are both unattached and have loads in common, walking, Meatloaf, reading, history,

Wales, we both agreed to reconnect and resume our fleeting friendship from A level Geography days. We are going to kickstart getting to know our adult selves by popping out for a drink on Wednesday in the Bistro Bar on the seafront!

Tuesday 11th June

11pm

Turned up for my cleaning job at Golden Pastures. I am a complete failure, so glad I never told Mam or Rhiannon about it, although I did tell Si that they took me on without even looking at my cv and qualifications, he was really impressed. My cleaning partner was a grumpy looking woman called Alice, she lobbed a brown overall at me and said, "Follow me" So I did.

Alice explained that we have to clean 6 rooms per hour, we just have to get on with it, no chatting with any residents we might bump into, because we are just cleaners and are not paid to socialise with the old people.

The first room is easy because the old woman who's room it is isn't there. Alice whips into action, she gives me a pair of rubber gloves, a spray bottle of orangey stuff and a j-cloth and steers me into the bathroom, which according to her is the best place for me to start. The truth is that after cleaning Uncle Albie's bathroom, this one is a dawdle!

Alice decides I'm already ok to clean on my own after my immaculate bathroom clean and so she points me to the next room and says "I'll see you in 10 minutes." I knocked the door and shouted, "Hiya! It's Arwen, your cleaner." Inside is Rose, she is 89, never been married, used to be a supervisor in the jewellery factory in Ton Mawr.

Rose said, "Stuff the cleaning, sit here with me and we can have a game of gin rummy, I insist." There we were, sharing a couple of my roll-ups, small glasses of sherry at our elbows, playing the hell out of gin rummy, when Alice after knocking politely on Rose's door and saying sweetly "Hiya Rose, have you seen the new girl?" took in the situation and marched me off to the manager's office.

And that's why I have been sacked. I've promised Rose to pop in and see her next week for another game.

Wednesday 12th June

11pm

Gareth and I had a lovely time at the Bistro Bar, we had loads to talk about and are going for a nice walk on Sunday then popping into the pub for a drink afterwards.

Thursday 13th June

11pm

Phoned Glenda to tell her I wasn't going to the Singles Nite! I told her about Gareth and me going to the pub instead, I thought she would be pleased that I had met someone but instead I got a lecture about dropping everything for a man and then another lecture about sisterhood. For fucks sake!

Phoned Gareth to rearrange meeting up on Sunday. He was fine about it and is coming to singles night with me and Glenda instead. Yay! He doesn't go out much because he gets accosted by people wanting mate's rates, and he is never sure if they are being serious. Luckily, I am not allowed to give mate's rates, ever since the incident with the collapsing table in 2009 and the protracted insurance debacle with Betty Upstairs' daughter.

Phoned Glenda to tell her the good news, she is pissed off about Gareth coming to singles night now, but I can`t uninvite him and anyway I don`t want to, so she is going to have to put up with it.

Friday 14th June

11pm

Mentioned to Si that Gareth was coming to the singles night with me. He is worried that I am giving Gareth the wrong message if I am interested in him romantically, by taking him to a place where the clue is in the name "Singles Nite!" I am touched that he is worried about me and to be honest now that he has mentioned it I'm a bit concerned too. I phoned Rhiannon and asked her what she thought, she said I was not thinking straight, that I should cancel the Singles Nite! plan and go somewhere romantic with Gareth instead, but I can't because of letting Glenda and the sisterhood down. Mam said "Stuff the sisterhood, what have they ever done for you, I fancy a carton of mild curry with my chips Arwen."

Saturday 15th June

11pm

My design your own Inspirational Bookmarks have really taken off, I have had to rent a table specifically for design and colouring in and have struck a deal with Glynys to provide the person doing the colouring in with a free tea or coffee (which I will pay for at the end of the day). It's strictly money in advance because that Moira from Richmond Cottages uses the blank bookmarks as a free activity for her kids otherwise. A free activity for kids is a good idea actually and I have already spoken to Si and Geoff about having a messy table in the corner, Si is up for it but Geoff and the cleaner are not so keen.

Nigel Next Table offered to sell me more £2 Pound Shop pencils, I thought I'd give him a chance to confess that he bought all his stuff at the pound shop and then just hiked the price up so I said "No thanks, got some exactly like yours from the Just a Pound shop, for a pound, you should pop in there, save you going to the wholesalers." He didn't even flinch, just looked at my pencils which were exactly the same as his, obviously, and said, "Nah, I'll stick to the wholesalers, better quality there."

Some of the commissions are not exactly what I would call inspirational.

Today's crop feature open coffins and a hangman's nooses and the words "Ask for forgiveness-not permission" and "Only the good die young" but my particular favourites are "God hates a coward" and "A coward dies a thousand deaths" these last two show God pointing the way to a very angry looking devil in the middle of a burning pile of logs.

Sunday 16th June

7pm

The general consensus around the dinner table was either I should not go to Singles Nite! or brace myself for the possibility that Gareth might have a "Love at first sight" moment with a tall beautiful single person with loads of hair. I think they were all trying to be funny, but now I am really nervous about tonight.

1am

Home from singles night, Gareth thought I was being a bit anxious as we walked from the car park to Ty Mawr, so I thought honesty was the best policy and told him what Si and the family had said and that I didn't want him to think I wasn't interested in him. He gave me a big cwtch right there and said "I`m so glad you told me! I was a bit worried too, I thought you had invited me along as a not very subtle hint that you were not romantically interested in me!" Phew! So he feels the same as I do, so happy about that! We danced all night, and even though Glenda (aka the sisterhood`s Welsh representative) was really annoyed with me, I didn`t give a damn! I`m seeing Gareth again on Tuesday night, he is coming around for dinner and is probably expecting something that doesn't involve tins and dried pasta. My efforts will be an interesting experience for him and a bit of a novelty for me. Asking Mam for a nice easy recipe.

Monday 17th June

11pm

The Lloyd twins, Rhys and Jac came in today, sporting identical sky blue ski jackets and aviator sunglasses, returning their work placement forms. Still identical then, I say, they identically sniggered like bloody 10 year olds.

Si looked up, said "You know those jackets come in different colours don't you boys, it's bad for your mental health to be so identical, I'll have a strong word with your mother if you like." They looked a bit miffed so I took the forms and sent them packing.

"They will probably set fire to the wheely bins now" I say.

Lovely text of Gareth to say how much he loved dancing with me last night, and that he was looking forward to dinner at mine.

Tuesday 18th June

11pm

I dug out the slow cooker and cooked brisket with shallots, carrots and mashed potatoes, Gareth brought half a bottle of a lovely red wine to go with the beef. Dinner was surprisingly good, the downside to this is, that Gareth now thinks I'm a really great cook! I'll have to come clean at some point otherwise I'll be so stressed out about lumpy gravy and oven times that I won`t enjoy my dates with Gareth. He had to leave early as he is conducting a big funeral tomorrow.

Thursday 20th June

11pm

I keep dreaming about Dai lately, I say dream, but really they are nightmares! Last night, I dreamt that Gareth and I were dancing to "Frankie and Johnny" when all of a sudden Gareth turned into a grinning Dai, he said "I`m not dead yet" and then shot me with a little silver gun. I woke up then nearly jumped out of my skin when the phone rang. It was Badger saying he had a window. "What?"

"For the shelves, I`ve got a window for the shelves!" finally worked out he has a spare hour when he can come around to measure up for the shelves! Monday at 6 0`clock he said.

Saturday 22nd June

Today`s best sellers at the craft fair were my new animal bookmarks.

"Never trust your dog to guard your sandwich"

"Every person is sociable until your cow invades their garden"

"A pig in a satin dress is still a pig"

Sunday 23rd June

7pm

Went for a bracing walk on the beach with Gareth after lunch. On Sundays I usually go home from Rhiannon's full of lunch and lie comatose on the sofa for a couple of hours watching terrible romances on the movie channel. So going for a walk with Gareth was a bit of a shock to my system, mainly because when *I* say walk by the sea, I mean a slow stroll by the water's edge and then a cappuccino in the Beach Hut Café at the far end. When *Gareth* says walk by the sea, he means something entirely different! The Beach Hut Café was behind us by at least half a mile before Gareth unpacked his rucksack and we sat down on the picnic blanket with a coffee and a cheese sandwich. I was shattered! My new walking boots were killing me but he has stuff to rub on them, he will pop it around to mine later and then we can both head off to meet Glenda at Ty Mawr.

I'm soaking my feet in that foot bath that has lived in peace under the stairs for at least a decade, while I write up my journal. I phoned Rhiannon for advice and it's definitely not ok to wear flat comfy daps to a dance, especially if you are short and middle aged.

Monday 24th June

11pm

Badger came around to measure up for the shelf, after a long discussion about how it would be better to take down the old shelf and then fit two new ones, so that they match, I left him to measure up and went to make us some coffee. Later, he joined me in the kitchen for coffee and the conversation turned to Dai and his disappearance. Badger said that he had something to confess! I was all ears! The Monday before Dai jumped off the Head, he turned up at the workshop with a brand new holdall, he told Badger he was taking up cricket which seemed odd to Badger as he had never mentioned being interested in cricket. But the point of Badger's confession is this, when Dai was out on a job and Badger was in the workshop finishing off a door, he took a look in the bag, it was full of new clothes and a massive wad of £20 notes! Later, Dai came back for lunch and said to Badger, "Have you been nosing around in my bag?" Badger acted all offended and said, "Why would I want to nose around in a load of cricket stuff!" and then stamped off angrily to have a smoke and to hide any signs of guilt. I was wondering where all this was going but then he came to the point of the confession. When he checked the following day, the holdall had been fitted with a little padlock and by the Monday after Dai had jumped, the bag was gone, he never told the police because it didn't seem important at the time. I thanked Badger and said that his revelation was incredibly significant, and that I would add it to my list.

He will be back to fit the shelves for free when he has another window.

Wednesday 26th June

11pm

I should never have told Si about how I'm going out with Gareth now, because he keeps asking stupid questions and has printed off things to ask yourself if you are going out with an undertaker. He shoved it into my bag and later on he sent me a text to ask if I had found it!

I`m sick of his childish jokes! He has another new girlfriend, this one works in the chip shop, so I`m going to bombard him with questions about chips until he stops going on about Death.

SIMONS LIST

- Do you ever wonder if the flowers he brings you are nicked from a dead person?
- Does he smell of death?
- Does he smell of embalming fluid
- Is he good at putting makeup on, painting your nails, doing your hair, undressing and dressing you?
- Are there dead people in his house?
- Are there coffin coffee tables in his house?
- Are there huge bouquets of flowers in his house?
- Does he do mates rates?

QUESTIONS ABOUT CHIPS FOR SI

- How many tons of potatoes are turned into chips every year?
- Can you eat chips for breakfast?
- Does your girlfriends flat smell of chips

- Do chips make you fat?
- Do chips give you spots?
- Are you sick of free chips?
- Are chips still vegan if you use lard?
- What is your favourite accompaniment to chip-shop chips?
- Are your mother's chips nicer?

Friday 28th June

8pm

Mentioned to Mam that I was having nightmares, she said it was a sign that I was unsure about Gareth, but I'm not unsure about him at all. I just need to get on with finding out what happened to Dai, and then he can bloody vacate the room he occupies, rent free, in my head. Off to meet Gareth at the Owain Glyndwr.

Sunday 30th June

My long walks on the beach with Gareth are so good for me. I think that walking is my new hobby, especially walking with Gareth. That's two things to cross off the list.

July

Onwards and upwards!

Intentions

Be nicer

Be more interesting

Find a new job

Be a better daughter

Be a better auntie

Write longer poems

Find out what really happened to Dai.

Crossed find a boyfriend and find a new hobby off my list, Yay!!!!!

Monday 1st July

11pm

Spent the whole day helping Glynys to set up an online account at the wholesalers, this is Geoff's idea, dragging our older staff into the 21st century. Maybe he should be the one who sits with her all day trying to explain how it works. To be honest I think she is being a bit computer illiterate on purpose because a trip to the wholesaler is the highlight of her week. I'm exhausted!

Tuesday 2nd July

4pm

Just found a book on Amazon about Dylan ap-Ithyll, the great Welsh free thinker and philosopher. How shocked am I! Book is called the rise and fall of Dylan ap-Ithyll and after reading the synopsis I do not feel at all guilty anymore that I used his book of daily affirmations (The Everyday ap-Ithyll) as a diary in 2009 and wrote all over it. Does that make all his thoughts about life wrong? I mean how can such lovely affirmations be the product of such a twisted mind? I suppose the truth is this

1. Even people who seem nice can be not nice.

2. Even not nice people can give good advice.

3 Thinking about this too deeply can give you a headache.

Thing is, can I still use his pithy observations about life on my bookmarks, knowing what a bastard he was? I mean, will *"Flow like a river, bend like a tree."* be empty meaningless words now, signifying nothing?

Wednesday 3rd July

6pm

Bumped into Jude Jones from Smuggler Street, in the Spar, she was buying jacket potatoes, I was looking for a nice cheese. She said Sherlock has opened a detective agency now, I said I was pleased for him as his special interest has always been Sherlock Holmes, the legendary fictional detective. She gave me his business card which I promised to pin up in the centre.

Sherlock Jones

Private Investigator

No job too big or small

11pm

I went to poetry group. I have fixed the March haiku, so I read the new improved version out to my fellow poets, they grudgingly agreed that it did now conform to the rules.

Searching for you still
Where the sun dies in the West
Grief rising like birds

Because my poems are so short, I have suggested that I could read another one, after a heated argument about how it was my fault if I chose to write short poems, it was decided that I could read one at the end if there was enough time left. Tamping!

Thursday 4th July

11pm

As I was pinning up Sherlock`s card on the local business board in reception, I thought maybe he could help me look for Dai, I`ll phone him later. Geoff the boss was peering over my shoulder as I did this. Everyone thinks he was something big in UNICEF or something, me and Si know that he was an accountant in Bristol who did a masters in Charitable Organisations and Not for Profits. He was in his usual bad mood, he is only here until he can put us on his CV and look for a job in England. He said "What is it with the Welsh and their nicknames? I mean Sherlock Jones! Really?" I thought 9am was not the time to give him a lecture on Patronymic stuff, but I typed up some info on it later and stuck it in his in-tray.

The Patronymic System in Wales

The reason for the prevalence of Welsh nicknames is because there are so few Welsh Surnames. The Welsh traditionally used Patronymic surnames derived from the father`s name. A boy would have the prefix ap or ab before his father's first name, meaning son as in Evan ap Rhys, girls used the prefix ferch as in Gwyneth ferch Rhys.

After Henry VIII broke away from the Catholic church in 1533, the Welsh legal system was absorbed into the English one and so fixed surnames became popular with the Welsh Gentry and eventually spread to the population of Wales as a whole. The consequence of this was that most surnames that then became fixed were based on the fathers 1st name, and the most popular names becoming surnames were Jones, from John, Williams, Davies from David, etc. Some surnames still have a trace of the Patronymic system e.g. Bowen, ab Owen, Preece, ap Reece and so on. This later led to a Victorian fashion in Wales for double barrelled names, Preece Davies being just one example. So this is the root of the Welsh love of nicknames, often linking their name to a profession as in Sherlock Jones or Dai the Death.

NB I hope you found this useful Geoff, if you google Patronymic names in Wales you can find some extremely interesting articles!

Arwen

Friday 5th July

6pm

I was sitting waiting for the fish in the chip shop and thought I could phone Sherlock and see if he could shine a light on Dai`s disappearance. I phoned and he has a spare appointment tomorrow evening. I won`t mention this to anyone, not even Gareth or Si because they will just try to dissuade me from going.

Saturday 6th July

11pm

Appointment with Sherlock at his office/front room went well, I took a list of everything I had learned and he promised mates rates if I helped with his Facebook page. Jude showed me into Sherlock`s study, it is completely jammed with Sherlock Holmes stuff, figurines of hounds with pipes and deerstalker hats, a whole shelf full of pipes and tobacco tins, a coat-stand with a load of capes. A very battered looking violin was attached to the wall above the fireplace. Amazing. I thought my collection of bird ornaments was obsessive, but Sherlock`s stash of memorabilia is something else. His bookshelves are a neat but eclectic collection of criminal activity - fantasy and fact.

I gave Sherlock the following list.

Facts

Dai disappeared on 3rd February at about 11pm.

No body

Sold important and treasured possessions prior to disappearing

Left his van outside Delyth's bungalow with the keys in it

Left three notes (to me, to Delyth and one by the standing stones)

Police not bothered,

Never used the word suicide or death in the notes

My mother thought she saw him in Marazion

Holdall full of clothes and money that disappeared from his workshop

Sherlock made some notes in his logbook and said he will get back to me as soon as he discovers anything of interest. He refused an advance because we are friends. I asked if I could borrow his Sherlock Holmes anthology, he was horrified! He said never lets anyone borrow his books because they were a crucial weapon in his arsenal. I was about to point out that Sherlock Holmes was a fictional detective but decided against it. Instead I asked if he used this particular weapon much. He snatched the book off me, dusted it down and said that I would be surprised at how important a reference book it was and that it was in constant use. Weird.

Now that I've handed things over to Sherlock, I feel as if I am moving forward with my investigation into Dai's disappearance.

Picked up Mam, Richard, and Gareth for quiz night, told them I am considering getting a job as a taxi driver, Gareth said not to bother as my car is crap. Charming!

Sunday 7th July

1am

Some people have moaned about me and Gareth going to singles night because we are not single, fair point I suppose, the women have complained that Gareth won't dance with them when they ask him and the management said it's not on as it gives the women confidence issues. No one complained about me not dancing, mainly because if I see a man approaching, I give him the death scowl while Gareth as usual just smiles politely at the women he refuses to dance with. I think it was Glenda who complained, even though we always sit with her and Gareth buys all her drinks for her, she makes little "Oh no thankyou Gareth," noises and then scared that he is wavering adds "Oh go on then, just a double gin please." He even does the odd dance with her, when her favourite songs come on and she sits there sighing.

I think that if it were possible, she would have just had me banned. She is such a cow, another one to delete from my friends list I think. I'll definitely have no friends left at this rate.

Tuesday 9th July

11pm

Popped up to Mam's with the sad news that her cousin Elwyn from the Rhondda is on his last legs and his funeral will be happening soon. As usual I used my key and shouted, "Mam it's me, Arwen!" To which she usually replies "Of course it is, who else would it be!" then we usually have a boring back and forth about killers who may have stolen my car or marauding rapists with spare keys, but instead of all this, she appears in the hallway and says, "I wasn't expecting you, what do you want, I'm really busy."

"Don't lie Mam" I say, "you are not very good at it, and anyway no one visits you anymore." I managed to squeeze past her and went into the sitting room.

Turns out, she has been mentoring Delyth who is searching for God! "How could you!" I shout, but according to Mam I'm out of order denying a fellow human being the chance to atone for their sins. Delyth says nothing, instead she sits there looking very chappely stroking a very shiny gold crucifix, balanced on her knees is a small New Testament and a plate of sandwiches.

"Go and make some tea Arwen, we are almost finished anyway." I nicked two of Delyth's sandwiches on the way to the kitchen, the looks of shock on their faces was worth it.

Mam said, "My daughter is not as nice as she thinks she is." After I had calmed down, I crept back into the sitting room and apologised for my bad behaviour, Delyth offered me the rest of her sandwiches which I refused obviously and Mam said she accepted my apology and would I like to join them in a prayer. What could I do? I knelt on the floor with them and mumbled amen after a prayer from Mam asking for God's help for sinners everywhere. So there it is, Delyth has found God, and Mam finally has someone to guide and convert and share the afterlife with, after giving up on me and Dad years ago. Turns out the cousin from the Rhondda was a nasty old bastard who bullied her unmercifully when they were children, so no great loss there for Mam, and not a tear shed, although she still wants to trek up to the mountains for the funeral, what is it with old people and insisting on going to funerals?

Friday 12th July

11pm

Took fish and chips and three balls of a lovely cream wool over to Mam's for her crocheted doilies. She took the wool off me, shoved it in the drawer and said it was too bland for her. I said "And here's me thinking that you used the bright pink and neon green because that was all you had." Her doilies have taken over the guest bedroom again, there must be about fifty of them now. I asked her if she would like to book a table at the craft fair, she said she would think about it. I said, "You could sell them and donate the money to the Food Bank, they would be really grateful, they will send you a thankyou letter that you can frame if you want."

She gave me a look, "Albie was right, you are obsessed with the Food Bank."

Saturday 13th July

Olivia, who kickstarted the revenge bookmark trend, popped in today and had a quick look at my bookmarks. As she was moving on to the next table, she imparted a bit more business advice.

"You should turn some of them into fridge magnets."

"Oh thanks Olivia, you should start your own business!" I replied. She came back to my table,

"You being funny?"

I genuinely wasn't but to prove it to her, I have now promised to go around to hers next week and show her how easy it will be for her to start a small business from home.

Sunday 14th July

At lunch I mentioned mentoring Olivia and asked for advice, everyone was very positive except Mam who said, "Is that Olivia from Richmond Square? Because if it is, don't go there on your own, she is a right bastard, even her mother won't visit her without a minder." I don't believe it! No one will go with me apart from Owen and Rhiannon was very firm about him *not* going even though he said he could film the goings on in case we needed evidence. So now I have to phone Olivia up and cancel the meeting! I was annoyed at Mam, but she said that was like being annoyed at the man who pulled you away from the edge when the London to Swansea sped through the station.

Monday 15th July

11pm

Phoned Sherlock for update, had to leave a message, as he didn't answer. The Lloyd twins turned up for work experience, they had ditched the ski jackets and had turned themselves into a pair of Emos, complete with black mascara and eye shadow. I don't know who started this annual work experience nightmare, fingers crossed they behave themselves, although they can`t be worse than last year`s crop to be honest, they couldn't string a sentence together and spent the whole week chain-smoking behind Pat Potatoes green beans trellis.

Phoned Olivia and apologised profusely for having to cancel our meeting, she said she expected me to cancel as no-one did anything nice for her, felt so bad I invited her to come to the craft fair next Saturday so that I could advise her in between customers.

Tuesday 16th July

11pm

Bronwen down the road, died today. I saw her yesterday, sitting out the front as usual enjoying the evening sun.

She was wearing a flowery dress and a pink cardigan and I told her she looked lovely. So it was a bit of a shock when her son Adrian popped around and told me the bad news. Died in her sleep, she was ninety-two. A good age although she and her family would disagree I expect. I offered Adrian a hand if needed, he said her house was rammed with years of clutter, so he would be around quite a bit and would let me know if he needed any help. This made me think I'd better get on with my decluttering, Owen, being the youngest of our clan, will be so pissed off if he has to deal with it all after I pop my clogs, and Mam keeps asking for her death book back and saying "I bet you've lost it!" I wonder if Gareth is doing the funeral. I could legitimately go along as a mourner because I am Bronwen's neighbour.

"Pop my clogs" I looked it up on google. So boring, I can't be bothered to write about it.

Thursday 18th July

11pm

Took Mam to her cousin's funeral in the Rhondda, my little car hates the narrow hilly streets and I mostly drive in second gear which annoys Mam and the drivers following me. The grey chapel was full of old people in black musty clothes. It was a nice service to be fair, it's hard to beat a chapel full of Welsh people singing hymns. The internment took place on top of the mountain, and I thought if you have to get buried, this is as good a place as any. Just bird song and the mountains for company. I might write a haiku about this. Mam and all the other oldies were in the pub drinking shandies and eating ham sandwiches, so it was very peaceful at the cemetery, the only mourners there were me and Alan, the dead cousin's son. Alan introduced himself to me, he was really nice, we had a chat about his dad, who apparently was the best dad a boy could have had. I didn't mention how he terrorised and bullied my mother, I think I can definitely cross being nicer off my list soon.

Friday 19th July

7pm

Because it was their last day, we gave the Lloyd twins a coke and a bag of crisps each and told them they could spend it playing board games in Uncle Bryn's Cwtch. When we showed them the little games room off the hall, they were so excited. Si and I congratulated each other on another Work Experience well done and we cobbled together a report on the Lloyd twins for Geoff and their school. Later though, about 1pm, they appeared in front of us, looking very sheepish, saying they had to go, we agreed they could leave early and thanked them for their help as they scuttled through the main doors. Si said his spider sense was tingling so we checked the games room, it was completely trashed! We video-phoned their mother from the middle of the chaos to demand the return of the twins so that they could clean up the mess, but she said it was our fault for giving them drinks and snacks full of additives and letting them play board games, all of which were banned from the Lloyd home because of the ensuing problem that followed when one of them cheated or lost.

You can tell she's a teacher can't you was the only thing Si could think of to say afterwards, "Oh aye" I said "only a teacher could look at the total fucking wreckage in Uncle Bryn's cwtch and calmly utter the words 'ensuing problem' bloody awful woman! At least they *didn't* set fire to the bins."

"Nah" says Si, picking up a broken monopoly board, "They never repeat their past misdemeanours, fair play, they prefer variety."

Glynys is really excited about the school reunion tonight, she is hoping to reconnect with some of her old classmates, I find this weird as she has spent her whole life in Cerrig-Mor. Turns out, there is just one particular classmate called Des Lewis who she used to go out with when she was 16 but who had to give her up and marry Eileen Collier because Eileen was pregnant. Eileen ran away to Newport a couple of years ago with the Asda delivery man and Des sank into a deep depression, according to his sister. Glynys thinks she might be in with another chance at happiness.

Our lovesick cook has decided to bite the bullet and rescue him from his gloomy life and has shoved the flier for the reunion though his door. On the back, she has written in very spidery writing," It will be nice to see you again Des, your friend Glynys."

11pm

Lifetime ban off the landlord of the Green Man, for sicking up on the new pool table, it wasn`t me it was

Glynys, I was just retching as I tried to clean the worst of it up with some paper napkins, to add insult to injury, she actually let me get banned and stayed there to enjoy the rest of the evening! I've unfriended her on Facebook and when I see her at the Craft Fair, I'm going to totally ignore her. I will take my own sandwiches and coffee from now on, that will show her!

Saturday 20th July

11pm

Glynys uncharacteristically turned up early to the craft fair. I ignored her attempt to apologise for last night's fiasco, but later on when she slyly placed a coffee and a tuna salad baguette on the end of my table, I wavered. She said while I was cleaning the pool table, Pat Potatoes, who was also at the re-union, was very solicitous and whisked her off to get a glass of water, and sober her up, then they got talking, she said she was very impressed with him, scrubs up well she said. To be honest, anything would be an improvement on ancient wax jackets, filthy bucket hats and wellies with the tops turned down.

The baguette looked delicious and I was starving as I forgot to bring sandwiches and a drink and Si refused to go to the café for me as he said helping middle aged women to feud was beneath him. So taking all the circumstances into account, I accepted her apology and her explanation for her behaviour and said I hoped she and Pat would make each other happy.

Olivia turned up, she brought some of the un-greetings cards she had been making. They were interesting cards, very alternative and niche I thought, so I convinced her to make a load more of them and then book a table as a trial and give it a go. As a confidence builder, I bought an overpriced card off her, the verse inside was quite funny, "If ex-friends were flowers, I'd put you in a vase with no water and watch you die!" She is ok when you get to know her. Still looks very scary though, I'm sure a lot of prospective customers were too frightened to come to my table. Even Si gave me a wide berth, the coward.

Sunday 21st July

11pm

What a day! It started with a phone call off Sherlock apologising for the delay and saying he had hit a brick wall and has concluded that everyone was right, Dai was indeed dead.

He said he wasn't going to charge me for the investigation and not to worry about the Facebook page as he was going to enrol on a course in Ton Mawr Tech to learn how to do marketing, but thanks anyway and sorry Arwen. I asked him if there was anything at all to add to the list I gave him, but he said he was really busy and had to go to his next assignment.

So that`s that then. Picked Albie up and headed to Rhiannon`s. Settled Albie into the living room with Mam and called Rhiannon into the garden to tell her about Sherlocks investigation, we had a little cry, then she called Richard and Owen into the garden to tell them while I told everyone else. Mam was very sad and gave me a cwtch, she said, "Put it all behind you now Arwen and concentrate on that nice undertaker man" which is probably the loveliest thing she has said to me for ages.

All Albie did was loudly demand a cushion for his seat, "I'm not getting any younger you know!" He seemed very agitated and I blame myself for dragging Dai's death up again, and upsetting everyone, I don't know how we got through lunch but everyone said things like "At least we know for certain now".

Later, after I had taken Albie back home, I took some flowers that I had bought from the Co-op and a very short but apt poem to read and walked up to Cerrig-Mor Head.

Farewell old friend
Fly fast, far, and high,
Be an everlasting show of bright lights
A million silver sparkles in our long
Dark nights

I stood on the edge, launched the flowers over the rocks and as far into the ocean as I was capable of and was about to start reading the poem, when I thought I wonder if the tide was in or out because no one would jump into the sea if all they could see was jagged rocks, waiting to skewer your body in numerous places leading to an agonising lonely death, it would be madness, the stuff of nightmares! Then this old bloke with a barking dog and a waving stick started shouting at me. "Get away from there! If you fall over it`s no end of trouble, I'll have to be a witness and my meds are due in a minute, you selfish bastard!" I said "My husband jumped off here, I'm just saying a last goodbye!"

"Shame on you then, you should know better, leaning over the bloody edge like that!"

So I sat on the bench instead and waited for the old man to go on his way. The poem seemed a bit pointless so I just went home.

I passed the old man on the way down. When he tried to keep up with me and have a conversation I said, "Sod off old man, I haven't got time to call an ambulance and wait around with you until the paramedics arrive if you have a speed induced heart attack!" and jogged the rest of the way home. I feel a bit guilty, what if I was the only person he had spoken to that day? Old people suffer terribly from loneliness, on the other hand, he is a miserable old bastard so is undeserving of polite conversation, a bit like me really.

I really thought that I would feel better because Sherlock had confirmed what everyone had been saying for months. That Dai was really dead, but I still don`t feel it, he is out there somewhere, I know it, I`m going to look up tide times.

Phoned Gareth to see if he wanted to come early to mine and share in my misery and continuing doubt about Dai`s demise, he said, of course love, be right there. He brought six bottles of Becks and his music compilation shuffle thing, lush! So the evening made up for the afternoon! As we can`t go to the Singles Nite! any more we decided to dance in my kitchen to my favourite Meatloaf CD.

22 Monday 22nd July

I stood in my kitchen this morning, making a second cup of coffee, watching Gareth sitting on the garden swing throwing bits of his bacon sandwich to the sparrows. I didn't think I would ever be happy again, but I am happy right now and that`s enough.

Tuesday 23rd July

11pm

Met Gareth for lunch at Luigi`s, went through all the evidence relating to Dai`s disappearance, it`s quite a lot, he agrees with me that something fishy is going on and that maybe some people have been feeding me red herrings! It feels a bit weird involving Gareth in my search for the truth about Dai, but he says it`s for the best because I am never going to rest until I have *found* the truth, whatever that is.

He reminded me how great we were on completing assignments together in school, oh love him, he is so nice. We are putting together a plan of action this weekend.

Before we both went back to work, we searched for the tide times for the night Dai is supposed to have jumped off the Head. High tide for that night was about 10pm, which I found disappointing but then Gareth pointed out that if you were going to fake your death, you would do some research because as I had realised, only a fool would jump into the horribly jagged rocks beneath the headland, you would wait for high tide and hope to be swept off to a watery demise in the ocean deep.

Wednesday 24th July

11pm

There was a meeting at the centre tonight, so me and Si set up the Henry Tudor Hall. It was about exploring a festival for the town, like Porthcawl`s Elvis Festival, Hay Book Festival, or the Brecon Jazz festival.

The Cerrig-Mor Goths and Emos Community group wanted a sort of day of the dead weekend, Si said "No" because its cultural appropriation but we could do a Halloween night dance instead. Si can be very dismissive sometimes when he is envious of other people`s ideas.

I suggested an Abba festival, honestly! So much groaning and negativity at this perfectly good idea! Si wanted a Star Wars extravaganza and had prepared a really impressive slideshow to try and convince the naysayers and moaners, and Edna from the launderette wants a cheese festival. I thought there were some really good ideas, especially if we could find a way to combine the Abba and the cheese one.

I made a draft flier to promote mine and Edna`s idea and left it on Geoff's desk.

Do You Love Abba? Would you die for a   bit of cheese?

If so, join us for a fun packed weekend of music and savoury eats at The Community Centre

(Fancy dress a must)

Merlin popped in briefly with a very colourful poster outlining his idea for a Fairies and Magicians fancy dress ball with a creche.

He wants a creche because he and Gwendolin are still having trouble getting a babysitter. I really like his idea, and will vote for it, in fact. It will definitely give my idea of a Cheese and Abba weekend a good run for its money.

Friday 26th July

11pm

Took fish and chips to Mam's, I mentioned Merlin's idea for the Fairies and Magician's ball, she started fuming and fussing about, wagging her finger in my face as if she was deranged! Apparently magic is outlawed by her chapel because it is against God, so she won't be going and isn't he the one who gave his kids weird unpronounceable Welsh names from the Mabinogion. She was going on about how I had weird friends and how it was probably him who encouraged me to buy the Tarot cards, so when she went to the kitchen to fetch two plates for the custard slices I had kindly brought to go with our fish and chips, I shouted through to her and reminded her of the meaning of "Barbara" I said, "Of course your name means strange foreigner, derived from the Greek doesn't it Mam?" That shut her up. She is very sensitive about her heritage, for the first 10 years after she moved here from the Rhondda when she got married to Dad, people were always saying things like "Not from around here are you" as if the Rhondda was on the moon. She looked a bit hurt so "Be nicer" will have to stay on my list.

Saturday 27ᵗʰ July

11pm

Met Gareth for a half of lager after the craft fair, we are working on the plan to find Dai. Gareth thinks that if Sherlock came so quickly to the conclusion that Dai is dead, then we should be able to follow his trail of breadcrumbs and find out for sure ourselves. This is the plan.

1. *Ask Sherlock for his investigation notes.*
2. *Scour the internet for news about people with amnesia.*
3. *Ask Police Officer Carys for help.*
4. *Get in touch with "Missing" charities for help and advice.*

Monday 29th July

11pm

I have so much to do now, I can`t keep up. Can I cross anything else off my to do list? Geoff said Si and me can go to the Porthcawl Elvis festival for information purposes, he listened to our argument that maybe the Hay festival or the jazz festival might be better, but he said the budget would only stretch to a day in Porthcawl with no frills, tight bastard. We Immediately set the intern to work finding out when it is and writing down where the best venues are. Si has promised not to drink if I drive and Geoff will reimburse me for the petrol and parking, but not lunch as we have to eat wherever we are, he said.

Wednesday 31st July

11pm

So, the intern has found out the date of the Elvis festival, there are venues everywhere, he said and the best thing to do, according to a report he read in the Vale Herald, is go to the town centre and soak up the atmosphere. He wrote the dates and all the relevant information on a sheet of A4 paper and we pinned it up on the corkboard behind our desk

August

Hope will give you courage

Intentions

Be nicer

Be more interesting

Find a new job

Be a better daughter

Be a better auntie

Write longer poems

Find out what really happened to Dai. Still not convinced that he is dead.

Thursday 1ˢᵗ August

Sort out spare room for Paul and Paula

11pm

Time for Paul and Paula`s annual free holiday at my flat. They are arriving tomorrow. All this is because of mine and Dai`s holiday in Tintagel in 2015 and Rhiannon saying it might be nice to look up a third cousin and his wife that she was still in touch with for Christmas card purposes.

Paul`s parents emigrated there decades ago to open a King Arthur Souvenir shop, which is still going strong. Paul is the manager now.

Friday 2ⁿᵈAugust

11pm

Paul and Paula are here. They brought me a gift from their shop, they have no guile or a shred of dishonesty between them, so the gift of a grey lamp in the shape of an Arthurian knight holding up a lantern was, said Paula, originally one of a pair, the other one was in the guise of a Lady, probably Guinevere, says Paul, "Shame I dropped it, slipped right out of my hands!" I said it was perfect as the one in the spare bedroom/study really needed replacing, Paula seemed a bit disappointed it was to live in the spare room. Sometimes with Paula you have to put your foot down really hard as she is a bit of a bossy boots, she was clearing spaces in the living room, placing the lamp there and saying, "What about here?" so in the end I had to take the lamp off her and plug it into the socket by the spare room bed, and then hide the perfectly good one that I had bought from Marks and Spencer's two years ago, in the cupboard under the stairs. Fuming!

I took them to buy sausage and chips for us all and fish and chips for Mam, she was great, she got out the best china and we ate in the musty old dining room which is only used for special occasions.

Later that evening, Paul was having a shower so Paula and me were having a cosy chat, she was so sorry about me and Dai splitting up and was saying she could not imagine life without Paul. I told her I was over it now and asked her what she thought of me going out with Gareth but Paula only wanted to talk about Dai. "Funny" she said "We thought he was in Tintagel a couple of months ago, looked exactly like him, maybe he was popping in to see us in spirit to say goodbye. Paul wanted to go after him but he had disappeared, well that`s what ghosts do isn't it?"

When I asked what he was wearing, she said "A very fetching pink polo shirt under a leather biker jacket and blue jeans which I personally thought were a bit too skinny for him, and one of those trendy grey man bags slung over his shoulder." Obviously, ghosts don`t have to wear what they died in then, either that, or it wasn`t him or he is not dead! This might be another clue, but what was he doing in Tintagel dressed like a trendy person?

Saturday 3rd August

11pm

Paul and Paula came to the craft fair, had their cards read with Trudy and stuffed themselves with baguettes and Welsh cakes, and bought a load of un-greetings cards from Olivia to sell in their shop! Later they trooped to the Garden Quiz with me and Gareth, we took ages to find a team name then that bastard Si changed it to "Death becomes Her" because he said I look a bit like Goldie Hawn and nothing to do with Gareth`s job. He is such a moron! Gareth didn't mind, he thought it was funny and much better than our original name of the Somerset Ciders, insisted on by Paula who as I've said already can be quite bossy sometimes.

Sunday 4th August

11pm

Paul and Paula and Uncle Albie and I went to Rhiannon's for Sunday dinner, she invited Gareth but I think our family is all a bit much for him sometimes. Mam was already there amusing Owen. Why are old people better with other people's kids than they ever were with their own? Paul and Paula get on really well with everyone as usual, and Owen loves them because they have a great accent. Rhiannon said remember you asked me to find out about that Asperger's Syndrome (Did I?) well here's some information, you could have done this yourself. She said she had given the printout a quick read through and had highlighted some stuff and concluded that I did indeed have Asperger's and that it would explain a lot. Didn't like to say it was Dai the Death's name I was really after so took the printouts and thanked her a lot. Stuffed them in my bag. I'll read them later.

Monday 5th August

1am

Paul and Paula came to the pub with me and Gareth, they spend the whole evening asking him about the more un-asked and delicate details about dead people. He was in his element and was making it sound more ghoulish than it is, in my opinion. Gareth obviously loves his job, especially when he has had a couple of pints. Back at ours, the conversation continued into the small hours, I didn't mind, it`s nice for him to have someone to talk to, his clients never have much to say.

I was in the kitchen, washing up the cups when Paula came up to me, gave me a cwtch and said that she thought Gareth was great and much nicer than Dai ever was. Bless.

Tuesday 6th August

11pm

Paul and Paula take me out for dinner to the new Italian as a thank you, they really do like Gareth, they think he is a star, and they hope he takes them up on the invitation to visit their shop soon, especially as they are expanding into gothic noir ornaments. I ask them if they are sure it was Dai that they saw, they are sure, both of them, the more they think of it, the surer they are.

Wednesday 7th August

11pm

I dropped off Paul and Paula at Rhiannon's for the evening, then went on to Poetry group, it was ok, I read my poem about the Green Lady, wish I hadn`t.

The Green Lady of Cerrig-Mor

The green lady only wears green
Her multilayered chiffons and silks reminiscent of a
small garden
Before the summer flowers appear
Today, her emerald green scarf sits nicely around her
shoulders, partly obscuring her gauzy blue green dress.
Even her stockings, well washed and thick have a look
of the mushy pea green about them.

But all her efforts are put in the shade by the neon
green trainers, her nod to the 21st century.

As I was reading it, Celia, the poet who is actually a poet and has had a book of poems published, said "It's about me isn't it? Your stupid poem!" She is often very rude because she is a published poet, and we often allow her a bit of leeway, but this time she has gone too far!

I was mortified and also offended at the same time, "You never wear green," I said, "You always wear purple! And my poem is not stupid Celia!"

"Pish posh" she shouted, "purple, green, it's still about me!" Well if the purple hat fits, wear it, that's what I think.

Next month, we have to write a poem about death. Perhaps I'll write a poem about a dead poet and her purple shroud.

Gareth came over after poetry evening, we cwtched up together and watched the Detectorists, I want one of those metal detectors, I'll put it on my Christmas list. I could start a club, rent a room in the Community Centre, I bet Si will join and Owen. It will be fun!

We haven't got very far with the quest to find Dai, dead or alive, but I am popping around to Sherlock's soon as he is not answering my calls, probably on a stake-out. Gareth is going to sweet talk Police Officer Carys about missing persons who want to be missing.

Thursday 8th August

1am

Paul and Paula's last night here so we took them to the Western Star karaoke night, Delyth was there with Les, so we invited them over to our table. Les said, glad you two are friends now like, I wouldn't go that far, but I smiled nicely at him. They got up and sang a duet, that lovely Barry Mann song, "Don't know much, and I know I love you," they were very good, people had tears in their eyes and the applause and shouts of "More! More!" was deafening! Les told me that Delyth and Dai were a mistake and she was really sorry for everything. The more I find out about Dai, the more I think we were a mistake too.

I have seen Gareth every day since Sunday!

Friday 9th August

11pm

Paul and Paula have gone back to Tintagel, their last words to me before they drove off after an early breakfast were "See you next year!" Took chips up to Mam's and as expected had to listen her criticising Paul and Paula for being who they are, they might be a bit odd but are totally harmless. She wonders if Dai's side of the family have a problem with feritily as they all either have one child or no child, I say you only had one child! She says, but that was through choice, I nearly died giving birth to you, and I have never been right since. God, she's awful. Set me wondering as to whether she might be right though, but in any case, it's too late for me. Can't work out yet if I'm sad or glad or a bit of both. Maybe I am more like Mam than I like to admit to.

Saturday 10th August

11pm

I take my journal everywhere I go now and took it out of my bag at the craft fair so that I could write a haiku for the poetry group in it because I have lost my £2 Pound Shop book that I bought off Nigel Next Table. Then lost my journal, found it underneath the desk in the foyer, asked Si if he had read it and as expected he looked offended and said "No, of course not!" Lying bastard, did think I could quiz him about stuff he could only know if he had read my journal, but I tell him everything anyway, so he will just deny reading my journal and say something like "You told me that the other day mun, when we were sorting out the out of date hospitality biscuits!" and it would probably be true. He successfully changed the subject by sharing his home made broccoli soup with me, it was delicious, he is going to ask his mother for the recipe.

Monday 12th August

11pm

Simon`s mother`s broccoli soup

Vegetable oil

Onion

garlic

Leeks

Mixed herbs

Diced potatoes

Knob of butter

Stock cube

Broccoli

Cheese

Cook gently to soften before adding stock, broccoli, and cheese

I don`t think Si`s mother is very good at writing down recipes, I've sent it back to her with some questions.

Simon`s mother`s broccoli soup/queries

Vegetable oil (How much?)

Onion (Big or little, diced, or chunky)

Garlic (Crushed or whole?)

Leeks (How many?)

Mixed herbs (Fresh or dried?)

Diced potatoes (How many? Cooked?)

Knob of butter (How big is a knob?)

Stock cube (Veg or chicken)

Broccoli (Is frozen ok?)

Cheese (Cheddar?)

Cook gently to soften before adding stock, broccoli, and cheese (How much stock?)

I showed the recipe to Gareth, he thinks a knob is a two inch cube, but hasn`t got a clue about the other ingredients. To be honest, I don`t think he is very good at cooking either, which is why, like me, he haunts the ready meal aisle, hoping for something edible.

I had called around to Sherlock`s house on the way home from work but he was not there even though his car was parked outside. I peered through the front window and thought I saw a movement behind his desk but it must have been his cat because even though I rang the doorbell a few times afterwards, no-one answered.

Tuesday 13th August

10am

Sherlock`s wife Jude, phones to say there has been news and can I pop in after work.

6pm

Popped into Sherlock`s about 4.15. Jude showed me into his office/front room. He obviously wasn't expecting me and looked really surprised when I walked in but Jude stood there in the doorway behind me, arms akimbo and said, "You tell her or I fucking will!"

So Dai is not dead! As luck would have it, Jude drove up to their house just as I was walking around the corner of their street, I didn't see her but she assumed I had been in to see Sherlock and was surprised to find him hiding behind his desk, she asked what was going on and he whispered "Has Arwen gone?" Jude then interrogated him until he gave in and confessed to his double dealings.

I`m tamping!!!!

Took Sherlock`s Log with me, when I left, I said "I`m having this!" and as I snatched it off his desk I added "I`ll have a think about *NOT* posting a bad review on your Facebook page." I gave Jude a big cwtch and thanked her for her help.

June 2019 The case of the disappearing carpenter David Price Davies

Client .... Arwen Price Davies

> **Brief......** Investigate the presumed death of her husband who disappeared Feb 3rd 2018 at approximately 11pm.

Facts

No body has ever been found.

Sold important and treasured possessions prior to disappearing.

Left his van outside the house he shares with Delyth his fiancée.

Left three notes, on the headland, with his fiancée and with Arwen.

Police still involved but not actively as no crime committed as far as they are concerned.

Arwen's mother thought she saw him in Marzipan, a small place in Cornwall apparently. Never heard of it myself!

Badger Evans found a "Going away bag" full of clothes and cash in Dai`s workshop.

Results Eventually traced to Penzance where he is now known as Michael de-Haviland and is temporarily domiciled in the Star of the West hotel with his girlfriend Maureen and their son. No further action required. Dai has asked that his whereabouts remain a secret and has threatened me with legal action if I don`t comply with this request.

Notes (For my eyes only!)

Started work on Arwen's request to find Dai the following day. I Followed Albie and his carer Ken into Maggie Stamps café after I saw them together in town and recognised Albie as Dai`s uncle, was just about to introduce myself and ask them if they had any idea about what was in Dai`s mind when he disappeared, when Ken started asking Albie about what was in the letter from Penzance. Albie answered that Dai sends his best wishes, says he is glad that Ken has settled in and he owes him. More chit chat, more information. Dai has changed his name to a really posh one and is living the high life in a big hotel. Spoke to Albie when Ken popped out for a *smoke, he was very forthcoming, I now have a name and an address. Oh, yes, Dai has also won big on the lottery, lucky bastard! Decided to leave before Ken came back to avoid suspicion.*

The hotel is more of a country house, five stars it is, with a jacuzzi and a swimming pool, he has invited Albie down for a few days in the penthouse suite, posh bastard. I am thinking, "Wow, saved myself some leg work here!" I also noticed that Maggie Stamps seems very friendly with Uncle Albie, they were having a loud chat about when she is off to visit Maureen. I gathered my things together and made my way out just as Maggie said "I`m going the week after you've been down there, no room for both of us at once," she said.

You've got to love a bit of serendipity!

The following day I drove down to Penzance, to The Star of the West country house hotel, and arrived about 2pm. Michael de-Haviland aka Dai was out, so I left the building and settled myself in the car with my sandwiches and my flask and waited for Dai to return. I didn't have to wait long, he turned up about 2.30 with Maureen and the baby. I called out to him and asked if he remembered me. Maureen said I'm off to feed the baby, don't be long, Dai sauntered over, smiling and full of bonhomie until I told him why I was there, then he got a bit nasty, threatened me with lawyers, that didn't work, then offered me £20,000 pounds to shut up! I had to accept, so he zoomed off in his flash car and got the money, in cash. I sat in the car and ate my sandwiches and waited. When he got back, he walked angrily over to me and said, get out of the car, then he took a selfie of us with me holding the cash and said if I ever see you again, you'll be sorry. I said "Don't be like that Dai, they are grieving mun! Why did it come to this?" And this is what he told me! I've condensed it down a bit, because a lot of it was irrelevant drivel and if you ask me, he is the author of his own misfortune! If you can call winning the lottery a misfortune, although to be honest, it hasn't brought Dai much happiness.

1. *Dai was having an affair with Maggie's daughter.*
2. *She got pregnant and moved away swearing her mother to secrecy about the pregnancy and everything. Dai waited a couple of months, used his pretended lack of work to save up money and then won the bastard lottery!*

3. *Faked his own death and moved away to Penzance to be with Maureen and his child.*

4. *His body was never found because he wasn't dead*

5. *Dai and Maureen kept in touch with Uncle Albie and Maggie, swearing them to secrecy with the promise of free holidays and cash.*

6. *Persuaded Ken, who is a cousin or something to be Albie's carer and keep an eye on the rest of his family, sweetened the request with loads of cash.*

He said he felt very guilty about what he had done to Delyth, Arwen, and his family, especially Rhiannon and his parents, but he was caught in a desperate situation, I said, "Well at least you are happy now, aren't you?." He didn't answer that question just repeated his threats and told me to fuck off! I shouted out to him as he was stamping back up to the hotel, "Oi Dai! Who knows you're not dead?"

He turned to face me and after a pause he said "Badger, Albie, Maggie Stamps and you, you bastard!"

11pm

After Sherlock`s revelations I went around Rhiannon's and said, "Brace yourself cariad" and then told her what Sherlock the Bastard Jones had found out and showed her the log. She insisted we pop around to Delyth`s and tell her as well. Delyth burst into tears and we ended up making her tea and then I took her back to mine for a bit, she was in such a state. It was more to do with him winning the lottery and not sharing it all with her. Called Gareth to tell him the news and he popped around with a bottle of medicinal wine and some snacks. Delyth got slightly tipsy and kept flirting with Gareth which really pissed me off, she also let it slip that the £20,000 in twenty pound notes he left in the teabag tin with a note that said, "Tell no one!", made sense now. I knew she was lying that day at Luigi`s! £20,000 seems to be Dai`s default pay off amount!

I hate it that I am beginning to think Delyth is ok really, the lying, marriage breaker is quite vulnerable underneath all that big hair and designer tops, flirting with any available adult, male or female seems to be in her DNA rather than an intentional act. Gareth thinks this is good and that finally I am seeing that Dai was the one who did the cheating, Delyth was just another woman enthralled by a man who was good at installing kitchens and whose personality resided in his trousers. I don't think he likes Dai very much.

I love Gareth.

Wednesday 14th August

11pm

Popped around to Badger's to confront him about Sherlock's Revelations, he was full of remorse.

I said "How much money did he give you Badger?" I thought he was going to say £20,000 but I was wrong, it was just a couple of thousand for a nice holiday in Türkiye! I asked Badger not to warn Dai that the game was up, he said he couldn't anyway because he didn't know how to get hold of him and didn't even know where he was, only knew that he wasn't dead.

I looked at him straight in the eye for an uncomfortably long while, he didn't flinch, I think he is telling the truth.

Thursday 15th August

11pm

Me, Delyth, and Rhiannon have decided to drive down to Cornwall and confront Dai tomorrow. Richard has booked us into a nice hotel with a bar and a restaurant, just outside Penzance.

Friday 16th August

9am

Gareth popped around with a load of sandwiches that Lucy, Gareth`s Dad`s carer had made for us and a huge flask of hot chocolate, he wished us good luck in Cornwell and invited me to stay overnight at his place next week.

Rhiannon picked me up at 11.15 am and we were off to Penzance. Richard had booked us all into a very expensive hotel, love him, and said "Go get him girls!" Rhiannon is driving because she hates it when I drive, and she and Richard have a better car, I am in the back, ruminating, Delyth is in the front, fiddling with the radio and pissing Rhiannon off. Delyth can talk for Wales. The journey down was straightforward enough, we stopped in the services in Somerset and then again on Bodmin Moor to eat the sandwiches that Lucy had made, Rhiannon snatched the bag off me and said "How many have you eaten already Arwen? I'm sure Gareth would have given you more than this! Look at this Delyth! She has eaten nearly all of them!" We arrive at the hotel at about six o'clock. Our family room has one single bed and a double, Rhiannon has bagged the single because she said she has special considerations being the driver and married to the person who booked the only available room left in Penzance, leaving her to load the dishwasher on her own and help Owen with his summer project on Catatonia. Richard had spent ages scouring the late bookings site.

I cornered her in the bathroom, do you really expect me to sleep in the same bed as my husband's mistress? She pushed passed me and handed me a pair of earplugs on the way, "You'll need these later, come on love, it's time for a couple of glasses of wine."

As we sat together in the lounge drinking wine and waiting for our table reservation to be called, I gave up on glowering at Delyth and Rhiannon, mainly because they were ignoring my bad mood, and decided to find out more about Delyth. She has had a sad life really, her dad left home to travel the world and have adventures with his mistress when Delyth was sixteen, (a very important phase in the father daughter relationship, said Rhiannon). Then she met a much older man, married him, got pregnant, lost her baby, her husband died of a heart attack, her mother had a fatal stroke, meaning Delyth at the age of twenty something was in the space of a year, grieving the loss of her child, her husband, and her mother! Poor thing, I went over to her and gave her a silent cwtch, which made her burst into very loud bout of crying. Luckily, the waiter appeared and after shooting me an accusing look which probably meant, "What have you done to this lovely person?" said "Your table is ready ladies."

1am

The reason I needed the earplugs and the wine is that Delyth can also *snore* for Wales, Rhiannon knew this because when Dai jumped off the Head and Delyth was in mourning, Richard and Rhiannon put her up in the spare room for a few days. I`m shocked! Don't be angry, Rhiannon said, you are nicer than that, we are all the family she has. I had a good think about things and to be honest, after hearing Delyth's life story, I have to agree.

Luckily, I have brought my journal with me, so I have something to do until I am so dog tired that the noise doesn't matter so much.

Saturday 17th August *Dai day, the bastard!*

8am

I have a list of questions for Dai alias Michael. Rhiannon and Delyth get exasperated with me over this, but I insist. Delyth says that was one of the things he hated about you, your lists. I add did you hate my To Do lists onto the end of my list.

My list of questions

How much did you win on the lottery?

Why did you pretend to die?

Who is Ken?

Is the baby yours?

Was the caterpillar in the Cauliflower cheese really the last straw?

Did you go to Tintagel earlier this year?

Do you hate my To Do lists?

10am

We have had breakfast and are ready to go.

11pm

The hotel was big and luxurious looking, we went into the foyer and from there into the toilets. Nobody stopped us which made us feel more confident. We decided that Delyth should saunter over to the desk and find out where Dai's Penthouse is. The man behind the counter is very young, his name tag says Jago. Do your best Delyth, we say. Rhiannon and I pretend to be interested in a carousel full of brochures by the lifts. Delyth is making good progress with Jago; he is definitely blushing at her outrageous innuendos and is giving her the lowdown on the best cocktails and the origin of the one named "Sex on the Beach." A tall skinny woman with sticky out ears strides past them, not even giving them a second glance, she looks very familiar and I nudge Rhiannon and point at the woman, who is moving in our direction. It`s Maureen! I recognise her from Maggie Stamp`s café! We step into the lift with her, she presses a button, "Floor 12, The Penthouse". Why didn't we think of that! "Floor?" She asks.

"Twelve" I say, Rhiannon butts in, "It's floor two" Maureen looks slightly suspicious and I'm afraid she will recognise us but I am hoping she is one of those vacuous young women who notices no one unless they are male, good-looking, and over eighteen. Rhiannon stabs the button for floor two and turns her back on Maureen. We hurry out when the door swishes opens and run back down the stairs to the foyer to rescue Jago and plan our next move.

Delyth was still flirting. Rhiannon said loudly "Hiya! I don't believe it! How are you love? We are just on our way up to see Michael in the Penthouse Suite!" (God, she's clever) Jago just looked a bit confused but also a bit relieved and decided to grab his cleaning cloth, ignore the woman with the weird accent and polish the desk a bit. Delyth had already whipped around and was saying "Well I never!" as she ran over to us and continued talking very loud nonsense as we headed to the lift, piled in, and pressed the button marked "Penthouse."

Rhiannon filled Delyth in on the Maureen sighting and then looked sternly at us, "Now remember girls, you might feel like killing him but he is my brother, we are just going to go into the Penthouse and have a civil conversation about why he did this." We promised to hold back.

Dai/Michael opened the door, his eyes widened when he saw us and he took a step backwards, lucky he did, otherwise Rhiannon's right hook would have been worse than it was "You fucking bastard bastard!" she said, so I knew she was really angry.

"Who is that?" Said a voice from inside,

"It`s us Maureen, Dai`s friends from Cerrig-Mor like" said Delyth, stepping over Dai/Michael, and then standing arms folded to watch the Dai and Rhiannon show. I helped Dai up while Rhiannon vented her anger and relief at him not being dead and then we moved into this vast room with views of the sea, furnished in white and silver, not my style at all. Maureen was clutching a baby, for protection I expect, not very bastard maternal!

Rhiannon rushed over and said, "Oh my God, look girls, he is the image of Dai!" He was and of course he is definitely Dai's son, I felt sick.

Dai said "I'm so sorry Arwen"

I wanted to be even more violent than Rhiannon but the baby was watching me so I just whispered in Dai's ear "I fucking hate you and your stupid ugly baby!"

Rhiannon had wrestled the little boy off Maureen and was introducing him, "Say hello to Auntie Delyth, say hello to Auntie Arwen" it was as if she was demented! "Ooh you're a lovely boy, gis a cwtch, gis a kiss, sws i mi!" she must be broody. I left them to it and went back down through the hotel to the carpark for a fag and a calm down.

Dai who had followed me said, "There's a shed in the back for smokers, follow me."

The smoking shed was very nice, with party lights strung everywhere and wicker patio furniture, I took a seat on a bench. Dai sat next to me. "You're a right bastard aren't you Dai," I said. He began to cry, noisily, I patted his back and said, "There there."

After a few more pats, I got fed up and said "Just tell me what the hell has been going on, we all grieved for you, except me that is, I knew you weren't dead, too bastard selfish I always said." Dai reached inside a big wooden garden box thing and took out a bag with a pouch of tobacco, filters, and papers, a lighter and a packet of polos, apparently he is not allowed to smoke, Maureen thinks it's disgusting.

I got out my list of questions, while he rolled us a fag each.

Basically, Dai had nothing much more to add to what we already know from Sherlock's log.

He *was* having an affair with Maggie's daughter who then got pregnant. Between then, they concocted a plan to get away from Cerrig-Mor and start again. When Dai won big on the lottery, it solved all their problems they thought, but as he found out, money really doesn't solve all your problems and it doesn't guarantee happiness. I was right all along His body was never bloody found because he wasn't dead!

He wouldn't tell me how much he won on the lottery but said it was loads! He is going to give me his share of the house, he will see his solicitor next week. He is so rich now, he has a fucking solicitor!

The baby is obviously his. He tried to implicate me in his dastardly scheme by saying one of the reasons, in fact the main reason he disappeared and pretended to die was because he knew how upset I would be about the baby, but I didn`t buy this, he always tried to get out of tricky situations by blaming it on me. I told him that I thought perhaps it had something to do with the flak about getting a woman young enough to be his daughter pregnant.

Ken, Albie`s carer was someone he knew from when he was contracting in Bristol he said, I told him that was a load of rubbish because Sherlock said he was a cousin, so Dai came clean and told me this long tale that sounded more fantastical than the lies! Ken`s son, Charlie, had found Dai on Facebook and he got to know Ken when he moved to Penzance because although Ken lived in Bodmin, Charlie and his wife lived in Penzance. When Ken lost his job, Dai asked him to go to Wales and look after Albie, who, when all is said and done, his father! I asked Dai why he hadn`t told us he was in touch with Albie`s grandson when he first found out before he disappeared. Dai said Ken didn`t want his mother to find out because she hated the old bastard. I asked Dai if he thought it was a good idea to let someone who had such a bad history with Albie be his carer, he nudged me and said "Two sides to every break-up Arwen! You know what I mean." Ken eventually agreed to go along with Dai`s plan, as far as Dai knows, Albie still hasn't worked it out, which I think is sad, time to right another wrong! But I`ll let Rhiannon sort that out.

He went to Tintagel because Maureen wanted to look at this amazing house but she decided against it because she thought there may not be any night life. When he spotted Paul and Paula he sprinted into an alleyway to avoid them. I asked him about the man bag, he said Maureen bought it for him to keep spare nappies and wet wipes in, and because she thought it made him look a bit younger.

The caterpillar was the last straw, he said. He has never been able to eat cauliflower cheese since and it is one of Delyth's speciality dishes, she puts little bits of smoked bacon in the cheese sauce. He is such a moron! He seems to think I did it on purpose and even accused me of buying a fake caterpillar because it was so green and still had all its legs.

He does hate my lists, especially the monthly his and her ones I used to stick on the freezer door. He said he never needed reminding to put the re-cycling out because I always did it. This could have turned into one of our re-cycling arguments but that`s all in the past now thank God!

Our last words to each other before we went back to the hotel were awful, he said he was truly sorry for what he had done and that life with Maureen wasn't as good as it looked, he missed Cerrig-Mor and his friends and family, and I include you in that Arwen.

I stood up "Well I don't miss you! You fucking Michael de what`s his name!" and stormed ahead of him, back to the hotel. Jago refused to let me in after a very angry phone call from Maureen had threatened him with the sack if he let any more Welsh people into the lift! Dai reassured him that he would not get the sack and I said just chuck him 20k I`m sure that would sort it!

"You are so bitter Arwen" he said

"And you are so FAKE"! I spluttered. After a silent ride in the lift we are back in the penthouse suite. Rhiannon and Delyth were playing on the floor with the baby, Madoc, and had been taking photos of him and each other cwtching him. Maureen stood sullenly in the corner, she beckoned Dai into the kitchen area, and hissed "Get rid of them!"

"Don't worry Maureen," I said, "We are going as soon as Rhiannon is ready."

Dai and Rhiannon put Madoc in his pushchair and went for a walk around the gardens. Delyth and I stood admiring the view from the window and tried to work out who Maureen was talking to on her iPhone, I thought it was her mother but Delyth said it sounded as if she was talking to a lover, because no-one calls their mother "Babe"

Later we sat in the car looking up at the hotel, Dai and Madoc were waving to us through the window, it was all mixed up emotions, Rhiannon was trying hard to hide her happiness at finding her brother alive and meeting her nephew, Delyth was fuming away loudly, using some of the worst swear words I have ever heard coming from the mouth of someone who looked like Barbie and who had just found God. I just wanted a fag, desperately. "Hang on I said, be back now" I ran around to the smoking shed and removed Dai`s box from its hiding place, I know this is really childish, I stole most of his tobacco, left an impossibly small amount in the pouch, along with one filter and a broken paper, then I left the matchbox with all the used ones in it and took the good ones with me! Sorted! Serves you right you bastard, Took the polos as well, feel better now. Gave Rhiannon a cwtch and told her it was ok to be happy and to be honest I am glad too that he is not dead, Delyth agreed, we all had a little cry. To lighten the moment, I told them about raiding the tobacco tin and then when they stopped laughing, it was polos all around to celebrate.

We called into a supermarket to pick up sandwiches and drinks for the journey, and then we were off home. I told Rhiannon and Delyth about going around to Gareth`s house and about how Si had made a list, and I was worried that some of the things he had written might be true.

I took the list from my bag and handed it over to Delyth who started to read it out aloud, but because they were both howling with laughter and Rhiannon was in danger of crashing the car, she had to pull onto the grass verge. I`ll never trust them to take my love life seriously ever again. I told them this and all I got in return was, "Oh, you old silly!" and "You are so easy to wind up Arwen!" I started to cry, so they both sat in the back with me for a bit and gave me cwtches and apologies, after a bit, I said, "Right, I`m ok now, I forgive you for laughing at me, let's get home for god`s sake!"

At various intervals on the way home, one of us would say "Michael fucking de What`s his name!" and we would all burst into laughter. He will always be Dai to us.

Sunday 18ᵗʰ August

11pm

Went to Rhiannon's for dinner and a de-brief, most agreed that Michael de-Haviland is a bastard, even though Rhiannon and Owen still love him. Albie didn't even pretend to be interested in the news about Dai and Maureen Dai running off, and said nothing when we told him that we knew that he knew Dai wasn't dead but that we forgave him because he was an old man. Richard looked as if forgiveness was the last thing on his mind.

Rhiannon is looking for the right moment to tell Albie that Ken is his son, the sooner the better if you ask me. She decides she will give him a lift home and have a quiet word with him and then Ken.

Went walking with Gareth later, filled him in on all the drama, he says "Well done, Arwen, you knew he wasn't dead!" I feel that I am so over Dai now in all respects and can get on with the rest of my life. If I had put "get a life" on my intentions list, I would be soon crossing it off!

Monday 19th August

10am

Rhiannon phoned me to say that she had told Albie about Ken. Albie just laughed it off and said he already knew, he had worked it out when Ken showed him photos of his son Charlie as a child, spitting image of Ken at the same age apparently. Ken had sworn him to secrecy because Dai wouldn't be happy about the news getting out. I asked Rhiannon if she was ok, she said she was, but that she couldn't work out how Dai had got into such a mess and had turned into such a stupid cruel person.

Rhiannon deserves better than this. In an effort to cheer her up I asked her if she would like to pop along to Maggie Stamp's Café with me to impart the good news! I'll be there at 1pm!" she said laughing. Can't wait to see the Maggie and Rhiannon show!

Told Si about Dai, he was shocked about the lottery money but really pleased that Dai was signing over the house to me. He said, does that mean you'll let me rent the upstairs flat when Betty Upstairs dies? Apparently his Mam won't let his girlfriend stay over and I agree with him that it's probably time for him to move out and that I will but also told him that Betty Upstairs is in good health and will probably outlive me. We then have a veiled request regarding the status of my spare room, but I said I was busy turning it into a walk in closet, courtesy of Badger, what a liar I am sometimes.

6pm

I left work and met Rhiannon outside Maggie Stamp's Café, we went in, sat down, and waited for Maggie to sidle over with her little note pad, all pink lipstick smiles and falseness! "What can I get you ladies?" she said, before I could answer, Rhiannon said, "The truth and make it snappy!" as she said this, she shoved a chair out, told Maggie to sit down and said to me, "Go and look after the counter my love." So I did.

Maggie Stamps was sorry about the lies and agreed with Rhiannon it was her fault for producing such a spoilt entitled daughter who went after attached men twice her age. Mind you, Maggie added that Dai`s recent penchant for women young enough to be his daughter was also a bit of a worry in her opinion. Rhiannon agreed with her and so it all ended well with free chips and half price cappuccinos. Rhiannon told Maggie she would look in the loft and find some photos of Dai when he was a baby and drop them into the café because Madoc is the image of him.

As we both stood outside, I thought, I`m so glad I persevered with all this because Rhiannon looked as if a weight had lifted from her shoulders, better to have a lying scumbag of a live brother than a dead one.

Tuesday 20th August

11pm

Went to Gareth's for dinner and "The Sleepover!" last night. The house is huge, we went first to say hello to his very old father who called me Kathy and kept saying they had run out of whisky when there was obviously a huge half full bottle of it on the sideboard.

As I excused myself to go to the toilet, I heard him say to Gareth, "Keep her away from the whisky for God's sake, we don't want a repeat of last time!" and Gareth saying quietly, "Her name is Arwen, she has never been here before!"

Who is Kathy? I'll ask Gareth later.

We were joined for a very lovely dinner, by Caradoc's live in carer/cook, Lucy Weekes, the PA is very beautiful is only about 24 and is clearly not interested in Gareth, (thank God because she is stunning and a very good cook, I'm very wary lately of unmarried women who can either cook or are beautiful and she is both) she started every conversation with "Adrian said", Adrian is her boyfriend, says Gareth.

After watching a repeat of the Chase, which Caradoc knew all the answers to (seen it before, loads of times, whispers Gareth) we say goodnight to the old man and head up the stairs.

Gareth unlocks a door to reveal a huge loft style apartment which, he told me proudly, he designed and furnished completely by himself! "So you live up here" I said, Gareth said the old man used to drive him mad when he lived in the main house, kept making him go out to check on the bodies and stuff! I must have looked horrified because he burst out laughing and gave me a cwtch.

"I'm joking, he only watches repeats of old quiz shows on the tv and he never stops talking. I have dinner with him every night and we watch the quiz shows for an hour, then I retreat to my lovely loft! Nice isn't it, have a look around." I think I have definitely fallen in love with Gareth, who would have thought this was possible, when we shared a desk in school all those years ago.

It was nice to spend such a long time not even thinking about Dai and being surrounded by our joint possessions. It set me to thinking that it was time for a big clear-out at my place. I'll have a good look for that Death Cleaning book that Mam loaned me. I asked him who Kathy was, she is someone he used to know. Someone from the past, he said.

Sunday 25th August

Dads heavenly birthday, so picked Mam up and off we went to the chapel to light a candle inside, then out to his grave to put some flowers on it. He hated flowers, she said, but what else is there to put on a grave? I said some people bring their dead loved one their favourite drink, they take a quick sip and pour the rest into the grave. Mam was shocked! "I don't know where you get these insane ideas from Arwen!" I pointed to a grave with some fairy lights, a pint glass and an empty lager bottle on it, but she wasn't at all impressed.

We sat there thinking of Dad for a bit then we had "The Conversation" about Mam's death. "Don't forget Arwen, to you know, whasname me in the same whasname with your Dad when I you know......." I move closer to her, "When you whasname, is it?" she sniffed, I gave her a quick cwtch, "Don`t worry Mam, I will."

Wednesday 28th August

11pm

Got a letter from Dai`s solicitors saying that he had signed over his half of the house to me, so that now I was the sole owner, and that Dai was filing for divorce as agreed by Dai and me.

Dai phoned me this evening to ask if I had got the letter and to check that everything was ok. I said everything was fine and it was good to move on with things as then he could marry the mother of his son, he was quiet for a moment and then he said, "And you can marry Dai the Death, once he has managed to get *his* divorce that is." I was speechless!

"Bye Dai," I mumbled, "Speak soon." What did he mean about Gareth`s divorce? I phoned Rhiannon for advice, she said, "Maybe he was married once, why don't you just ask him? I can`t understand how you can be going out with Gareth for months now and never talk about his past!"

Thursday 29th August

11pm

Told Gareth how excited I was about my impending divorce, that it felt good to be getting free of someone you didn`t love. He said he was sure it was and changed the subject by saying "I can`t believe the old sweet shop is closing! Town won`t be the same without it!"

Friday 30th August

11pm

Mentioned to Mam that Dai said Gareth was married, she said she always thought he looked a bit shifty and I should drop him, like a ton of bricks. He is not shifty! Although when my divorce was mentioned he did look a *bit* shifty. I am not dropping him though, he will tell me in his own time. Dai might have just been lying, trying to cause trouble.

Saturday 31st August

11pm

Bank holiday weekend, so we crafters were hoping for a bumper crop of customers. Trudy came and sat by me at my table and asked how things were going, I said great, those cards I chose were brilliant, she looked taken aback, she said "They were?" She ran back to her table and came back with the tarot pack and asked me to shuffle the pack and choose the cards for myself, I thought this was a bit mad but I did as she asked, four cards and one for luck.

> *Ten of swords*
>
> *The fool*
>
> *The tower*
>
> *Ten of cups*
>
> *The Empress for luck*

Ah she said, I see now, apparently I got it all wrong. The *first* spread was not for me but for someone who had caused immense sadness in my life, someone the spirits had wanted me to know about but unfortunately I was in so much of a rush that Trudy didn't finish the reading. This other someone was now on his way out, but was also back again soon, according to the spirits, whispering in her ear.

All this totally confused me. Trudy explained it to me again. This *new* reading shows a separation, then a new beginning, and an end to all that had gone before, a loving relationship and finally marriage. I'm still confused, but it sounds as if the first reading was all about Dai and todays reading is all about me and my life.

How come they are so similar I asked, and how come I thought the first lot was so good for me? She shrugged her shoulders, "Why would they not be Arwen, you take from the cards what you want, what you need to hear. She looked at me intensely, but this is another path, a good one, stay on it!"

I thanked Trudy and said I could see now what the St Michael card was about, Michael aka Dai and St Michaels Mount! She looked a bit phased out about that and after a long pause said she had no idea what I was talking about.

Later at home, I got out my Tarot pack and the book and looked it all up, the first reading and the second, wow, she is so good! I wish I hadn't spent the last couple of months trying to avoid her!

First reading (Could be Dai's but definitely not mine)

Nine of pentacles - prosperity, material wealth, security (Lottery win)

The fool – new beginning, opportunity and potential (Jumping off the cliff maybe)

The tower – allows you to tear down and start again in a direction you would previously never dared to consider (The move to Penzance)

The lovers – this card is all about choice, and summons up idealised visions of love, often based on infatuations and lust. (Dai and Maureen)

Second reading (mine)

Ten of swords-a terrible separation

The fool-new beginnings and opportunities

The tower-tearing down and starting again

Ten of cups-a fortunate marriage, contentment, a very positive card

The Empress-kindness understanding, feminine aspect, marriage.

I`m not going to mention divorce to Gareth again, I`m going to give him time to bring it up himself, because, if Trudy is right, we will be getting married soon! A summer wedding would be lush!

September

Live in the light

Intentions

Be nicer

Be more interesting

Find a new job

Be a better daughter

Be a better auntie

Write longer poems

Well, I have found out what happened to Dai, the bastard! So he is off my list at last! In more ways than one!

Monday 2nd September

7pm

Loads of people want to come to the Elvis festival with us, so Lizzie the cleaner is taking names and organising a coach because her son works for a tour operator, me and Si are a bit worried about this but at least if it all goes wrong with the transport it won't be our fault. I run it past Geoff and he said "Do what you like, you always do anyway" so coach trip is on! Si is pleased because his promise not to drink only applied when I was taking the car.

Gareth is picking up a Chinese Take-Away and then we are going to binge watch "Killing Eve" lush!

Tuesday 3rd September

11pm

Welsh Rarebit Day, I love cheese and Welsh Rarebit is the king of foods! Or the food of kings? Or maybe it's crumpets? Which are also very nice. Popped into work so that Si and I could make cheese on toast and invited Geoff to have lunch with us, to celebrate Welsh Rarebit

Day. He wanted to know why we were buttering him up! He is such a difficult man!

Gareth still hasn`t mentioned his marriage, I occasionally talk about how glad I will be when my divorce comes through and how great it will feel to be free, Gareth agrees, gives me a little cwtch and then changes the subject. I'll definitely tell him what Dai said next week, the thing is, maybe Dai was lying, and Gareth is not married. The only person he has mentioned from his past is a girl from England that he went out with when he was at university. But then he goes quiet and says he doesn`t want to talk about it, because that part of his life is over since he moved back to Wales to take over the business. Last night after dinner, he looked very thoughtful, then he asked how I can be sure that my feelings for Dai are in the past, and so I told him. I have known Dai all of my life, he was my best friend`s big brother and Dad`s apprentice and looked after Mam when she fell apart after Dad`s death, so I will never hate Dai, but I would never want to go back to the life I had with him either. Then after a long pause, he says, I suppose that if you are a nice sort of person, it`s hard to hurt people you have loved, even if you don`t love them anymore, I'm not sure how that remark was relevant to me and Dai, perhaps he was talking about himself. I didn't question his remark, I should have, I just agreed with him. But then felt I had to add, just to make things clear, that I don't think I hurt Dai, in fact it was the other way around.

Wednesday 4th September

11pm

At Poetry Group I read my poem about death. Tried really hard to make this a good one to annoy Celia who was still very angry about my green lady poem and had said as I was packing up last month, "The poetry prompt should be right up your street Arwen, you are obsessed with death, maybe that's why you are so enamoured of the undertaker."

On other days

I think of you all

Careering around the universe

Visiting heaven's wonders, heavens curious edges

But today is not one of those other days

Today, I look up and see the dark

Clouds as grey and unyielding as my grief

More like a badly constructed obscenely long haiku said Basil whose terrible poem about death is titled, "How doth the sun get up in winter" and runs to a hundred stanzas. Although his does rhyme to be fair. None of mine rhyme unless by accident. Basil has a touch of the Dylan Thomas about his voice, he takes full advantage of this by speaking very slowly and deeply in a booming West Wales accent. Still fucking boring though.

Saturday 7th September

11pm

Very quiet at the craft fair, persuaded Si to get a tarot reading. He wouldn't tell me the results, but it doesn't matter I'll get it out of him next week.

Quiz night was great, our team came second so we get to choose the theme for the fifth of October, which is the last one for this year. We ended up choosing "Under Milk Wood" (which in my humble opinion gives everyone a good chance as they will have a month to read the play and swot up on it) and ignored the sighs and the swearing at our choice as we made our way triumphantly to the front to pick up our prize for coming second, which turned out to be the horrible tin of shortbread biscuits which I had donated to the foodbank months ago.

I've got my own little drawer and some wardrobe space at Gareth's now! I'll have to clear a space in my bedroom for him.

Sunday 8th September

11pm

Me and Gareth were on the way back from our beach walk and picnic this evening, it was so lovely, the sunset was amazing. Gareth held my hand and we told each other wild stories about the wreckers. We both had wet feet from the incoming tide because we were walking along the waterline. I think it was the sun and the water and the tales of wreckers. I thought about Ross and Demelza Poldark strolling along their beach, him broody in his dark cape, her wearing her emerald dress, hitched up to save it from the sea, and that's when I looked at Gareth and said, "I love you"

Oh crap!

"What?" said Gareth just as I accidentally on purpose tripped over a conveniently placed rock and fell dramatically into the surf. Not only was it wet but it was fucking freezing, bastard Atlantic! But the distraction worked and I saved myself from humiliation by having to repeat my declaration of love, because we ended up with him helping me up and wrapping the picnic blanket around me to keep me warm. So the moment had passed. Later at my place, Gareth seemed very quiet, he said he was tired and went home early.

Monday 9th September

Gareth has had to go away, so I have found the death cleaning book and have started decluttering.

Thursday 12th September

11pm

I've had a very stressful week. Gareth is still away, I don`t know where exactly, he said he needed to pop off to England to sort something out urgently and he will be back soon. Every night he sends a message saying goodnight and see you soon with a funny meme. I reply with loads of kisses and cute photos of me in the garden.

I think it`s because what I blurted out on the beach. He didn`t even say goodbye properly before he left, just sent a text cancelling our usual Monday night date. What have I done!

Friday 13th September

1am

Gareth was waiting for me outside the flat when I got back from work. He was holding a bunch of red roses and a bottle of wine.

I said, whatever it is you have come for, make it quick, Mam has to have her fish and chips by six o`clock, he said, "Oh I forgot about fish Friday! Can you phone your mother and tell her we will be late and that I`m coming with you, if that`s ok."

I shoved away the roses he was trying to hand me, "Where have you been? I am trying right now to be cool about it Gareth, but I thought it was all over between us! Oh, and by the way, I hate red flowers!"

He took my keys off me, opened the door, and said, "Phone your mother! I hope it`s *not* over between us, or I`ve just wasted the whole week!"

Phoned Mam, she said, "Oh don't think about me, starving to death," I mentioned Gareth was coming as well so she cheered up then and told me to remember the mushy peas and the lemon this time, and she fancied a can of coke.

He said, "Remember on the beach you said you loved me and then fell accidentally on purpose into the sea? Well, there is something I haven't told you, I hope to God you will not be too mad at me Arwen." Then he began a very rambling tale of being married in haste, to an older woman he met in Southampton. She is something big in Southern Celebrants, whatever that is, so the mystery of Kathy and the whisky is solved. The night Kathy decided to leave Gareth, she got very drunk first on his father's best whisky, and then told him she would rather die than move to Cerrig-Mor and their morgue of a house. She said she was going home to Southampton and will expect him to go back to her once his father dies and he can sell the business. I was so shocked, I just sat there open mouthed and speechless, you look like a fish, he said. You will look like a battered fish in a minute I replied.

Gareth held me close to him, "Oh Arwen, I am so sorry, I`m not going back to Kathy! I went to tell her it was definitely over and I want a divorce." He decided to go to Southampton and thrash out the details in person, rather than tell her over the phone because he knew she would kick off and hang up on him. Driving down there turned out to be a good decision for another reason, because the door to their house was opened by a very fit young man called Harvey, who was keen to let him know he was Kathy`s live in boyfriend and was a bit miffed when Kathy asked him to bugger off while she and Gareth sorted stuff out. "Don`t take any nonsense babe" he said, shooting a threatening stare in Gareth's direction as he headed up the stairs adding unnecessarily in Gareth`s opinion that he would be upstairs in their bedroom.

"Bit young isn't he?" was Gareth's opening statement and it all went downhill from there. Eventually Kathy agreed to the divorce, but wanted to arrange mediation first, she offered to move to Cerrig-Mor and help him with his dad, he said "No, and what about Harvey? Anyway, It`s over between us, has been for a long time and I've met someone else, I love her and I want to marry her."

When he told me this part I looked him in the eye. "Do you want to marry me?"

He said "Who else is there Arwen?" he got down on one knee and said "Will you marry me?" I said yes, obviously.

Kathy had said she would take Gareth to the cleaners, but eventually she calmed down and said he could stay in the spare bedroom so he could pack up the rest of his stuff and arrange appointments with some solicitors that they both knew to sort out the divorce, on grounds of incompatibility or something similar.

"How did that work out?" I asked, he went a bit quiet then and said he was glad there was a bolt on the spare room door and he was just relieved to get back home in one piece and with his stamp collection and his very expensive telescope. Hmmm!

So now we are both waiting for our divorces so that we can get married. What a laugh!

Saturday 14th September

Owain Glyndwr day, the last true Prince of Wales.
Twsog Cymru

11pm

Everyone is really pleased about me and Gareth, Si wants us to have an engagement party at the centre, he wants to be in charge of organising it as an engagement present. I tell him that we will think about it, but we have already decided that we will have it at Gareth`s place.

His dad will find that easier to cope with, and Mam and Si would love a nose around the house and gardens, looking for dead people.

Sunday 15th September

11pm

No further news from Dai about the divorce. Everything has gone very quiet, the only exciting thing happening is the news about me and Gareth.

Mam and Dad Davies have got over the shock that Dai is not dead and have resumed their weekly lecturing phone calls to him, they told Rhiannon that he hasn't talked about his disappearance much and instead tells them about what Madoc is up too. It's Madoc's first birthday soon.

Friday 20th September

11pm

Bumped into Alison in the chip shop, she said she was off later to a meeting about the re-established writer's group, which *she* would be running from now on. She said she would phone with the time etc and she hoped I would come along even though I was writing poetry now instead. Alison said she knew Stewart who ran the poetry group, that he was very nice for a poet and anyway, the writing group was only once a month on a Friday. The first one is in October, so plenty of time to string a few words together, she said. I gave up and said of course I'll come, secretly hoping that it would be on a night when I am doing something else. I gave up on the writer's group ages ago because it was so boring, and nobody liked what I was writing. Even though I moan about Poetry Group, I would miss not going, I have never felt like that about the writing group.

Googled celebrant, it's a person who organises a funeral, usually instead of a religious person, maybe I could retrain as one, seems quite an interesting job, according to Google. I'll do some more research, anyone can do it according to Celebrants Inc. (UK division) I asked Gareth what he thought, he said "Yeah, you can work for me love!" Rhiannon said that it would be nice because I know loads of lovely things to say from the bookmark business and Si said, it would be great because I look fabulous in black, all very positive, needs more research. I told Mam I was thinking of becoming a celebrant, she said it would suit me down to the ground because I was an irredeemable backslider and it would be nice for the unrepentant to have a fellow sinner to do their funerals for them.

I worry about her sometimes.

Sunday 22nd September

11pm

Had a lovely lazy Sunday with roast chicken for lunch and then our usual walk on the beach. It's Richard and Uncle Albies birthdays soon, so we decided to go to a nice Chinese restaurant next Sunday because Richard loves Chinese food and Albie moans about every restaurant we ever take him to, so to be honest, we didn`t even consider him when choosing where we were going.

Sunday 29th September

11pm

Went to the big Chinese restaurant in Ton Mawr to celebrate the birthdays. I bought Albie a nice warm hat, scarf, and gloves combo, he actually had tears in his eyes as he tried them on.

Richard got a book token and a bottle of nice red wine, he is so hard to buy for! It was strange having Ken with us and really nice getting to know him, he is a very interesting person. Uncle Albie sits there looking proud and takes all the credit for how Ken has turned out which is a bit of a liberty really considering how he wasn't around for most of his son`s life.

October

Be kind

Intentions

Be nicer

Be more interesting

Find a new job

Be a better daughter

Be a better auntie

Write longer poems

Wednesday 2nd October

11pm

Exciting news at poetry group, Stewart thinks we should publish our poetry in a little book! We have to submit three poems each by the end of the year, then next year we will get them published and can recover the costs by selling the little books to our friends and family. I will have to sort through my poems and pick the best ones, this one, the one I read tonight, "The Gutter" is definitely going in.

Playing with friends

In a gutter

In the rain

In boots that leak and a yellow

Fisherman`s hat

Damming up drains with

Stones and weeds.

The life of a sailor in a

Small Welsh street.

Celia says if I submit my poem about the green lady, she will sue me.

Friday 4th October

11pm

Si and I have realised that the Elvis excursion is going to clash with the last quiz night, never mind, we can do it, Gareth says he will pick me up at 7pm and then drop around and pick up Richard and Mam, should be back from Porthcawl by about 6pm I hope.

Saturday 5th October

Elvis festival Yay!

11pm

Back home after an exhausting day searching for the Elvis Festival and then having to attend the last Quiz in the Garden, we actually won the quiz but that didn't make up for a terrible day in Porthcawl!

Sunday 6th October

11pm

The terrible day in Porthcawl started early outside the community centre with me and Si herding ridiculously dressed people onto the coach which was leaving at 10am. I was the only one not dressed up because I didn't want to and was representing our town and the community centre and was planning ahead for the quiz night, Si said he wasn't bothered and would quite happily wear his Elvis costume to the quiz, yes, well, I knew that. I wore my community centre anorak and my lanyard and was hugging a clip board so no one could fail to see that I was in charge. By the time we arrived, Most people had already started on the lager, when I pointed out to them that drinking before lunch was bad for you, they just put on stupid voices, saying things like " Oh, la de da, no drinking before luncheon, everyone!" so they were in good spirits as we parked in the town car park, which was surprisingly empty and looked depressing in the drizzle.

That bastard intern had got the dates wrong, it was last weekend. I'll be having a lot of very sweary words with him on Monday, he is lucky I haven't got his phone number with me now because hopefully I will have calmed down a bit by the time I get to work. We cheered the Porthcawl townspeople up though, a busload of tipsy Elvie's and a very grumpy little woman in a navy anorak, wandering around looking for the music, and complaining that it was a bad show. We traipsed up the high street, taking in the forlorn remnants of the festival, a bit of bunting here, a flapping poster there. Finally, we invaded one of the pubs and after hearing our story they dug out some Elvis cd`s and gave us free coffee, they were really nice to us. One of the bar staff, a lovely man called John, had a cousin who was a top Elvis impersonator, so he phoned him, explained our predicament and Elwyn Tender who lived just down the road turned up in full clean but very rumpled Elvis regalia which he apologised for by explaining that his Mam hadn't got around to ironing it yet, and gave an impromptu concert. He also gave me and Si loads of tips for a successful day for our own festival, so it all ended well. I suppose.

Lizzie our cleaner was tamping mind. She had ordered her land girl costume online and it had cost a fortune, we took a photo of her with Elwyn to cheer her up. Then we had group photos with Elwyn and the bar staff which Si posted on the community centre Facebook page.

As usual, I was the cause of hilarious jollity at the Sunday lunch table, "Our lives would be so boring without you to cheer us up." said no-one in particular out loud, but I could tell by the number of times Elvis, his play list, and Porthcawl cropped up in the conversations over the roast chicken and broccoli. It started with Rhiannon asking me to pass the "Blue suede shoes. Oops! I mean gravy!" And Richard replying "Don`t be cruel!"

Monday 7th October

11pm

By the time I got to work, Si had already printed off the photos of the Elvis trip out and was arranging them in the glass display board opposite our desk, where everyone could see them. I insisted he remove the one of me looking grumpy and clutching a bottle of cheap vodka, which, to be clear, I was holding for Beth from Fisherman`s Walk, who was in the public toilet by the carpark at the time.

I had typed up in list form, the tips that Elwyn Tender had given us, hoping this would help if Geoff called us into the office to sack us for incompetence. I also googled "Organise a town festival," what a rabbit hole that was!

Review of the Trip to Porthcawl on October 5th

Simon and I interviewed a very successful Elvis Impersonator who gave us the following tips for a vibrant town festival, although these are specifically for the Elvis Festival in Porthcawl, we feel they can be adapted for our own event and will result in a very successful weekend of activities.

- Advertise extensively.
- Order your Costumes in time.
- Check out venues personally before the day to ensure they follow Health and Safety rules
- Check the audio equipment.
- Set up social media pages
- Inform the Police and emergency services and get the event licensed

Our interviewee (Elwyn Tender) has given us his details and is available for further advice

****

I know this list is a bit lame, but at least we tried, I had picked up a load of leaflets etc from the tourist information office in Porthcawl so I put them, the list and a rather battered leaflet I had found in the public toilets, (it was a bit wet, but luckily the hand drier sorted it out) in a zip lock A4 folder along with Si`s photos.

I had intended to sneak them into Geoff's office before he got to work, but too late. I had knocked on his office door out of courtesy, and entered expecting the room to be empty, Geoff was sitting at his desk, he said "Oh! Arwen! Take a seat." My eyes took in the paper bag and the takeaway cappuccino from down the road. He took the folder off me and quickly scanned the contents.

"I will say this for you and Si, you both have the ability (Or cunning) to turn any size disaster into a seemingly competent event. He looked me straight in the eye "Jungle drums," he said, tapping the empty paper bag. (Bastard Elvira from the coffee shop, that`s the last time she comes on a trip to Porthcawl with us) I was mentally composing a letter of complaint for unfair dismissal, when he burst out laughing (a first).

"I mean, look at this!" he was holding up the photo of me and Si in the pub, eating pie and chips (Si was wearing his Elvis wig and Elton John sunglasses).

"And this!" he waved the old leaflet at me, "It's got a boot print on it!"

I stood up, "Please don't sack Si, he will never get another job, you can make me the scapegoat and sack me if you like" then I burst into tears.

"I've had a terrible weekend, herding them all around, I was the only sober one there except for the coach driver, putting up with all the complaints, the constant moaning, and it's all because of that bastard intern Whatshisname from Head Office's fault!"

I was so embarrassed by my outburst especially as he rushes around to where I stood, gave me the napkin from his iced doughnut to mop up my tears with and said soothingly "There there Arwen, I'm not going to sack you! I'm not a monster, you know!" Fortunately, he has never had any intention of sacking us because he doesn't think he could possibly replace us. Turns out, he quite likes us even though he never gets invited to any out of work events we organise. He said he has come to terms with our glaring inadequacies and weighed them up against our extensive knowledge of the town and the head office politics. I told Si and we are both wondering if we can take this as a compliment and decide to invite him and his wife to the Halloween pub crawl. We will leave the invite as late as possible, so he has trouble arranging childcare. Phew, what a relief!

Phoned the intern, he didn't answer, so left him a message to call us asap. To be fair, he phoned about an hour later and told us he had muddled the dates up with a Glamping Gamers weekend that he was trying to secretly book on Geoff's computer for the 4th to the 6th of October. He was very apologetic and didn't realise until he saw a news article last Wednesday about how successful the Elvis Festival was, but didn't like to tell us, because he was a bit afraid of me after the problem with Geoff giving him my computer for the day. "That will teach you to be mean" Si said, "Karma for all the rubbish jobs you made him do."

I think he did it on purpose to pay us back for not inviting him to quiz in the garden, I wanted to invite him but Si thought he was always trying to chat up his girlfriend, so banned him by saying interns couldn't attend. Anyway, all's well that ends well. Going to cross "Get another job" off my list. Geoff is beginning to grow on me.

Thursday 10th October

11pm

Found myself looking at birthday cards for one year olds for Madoc's first birthday tomorrow, but I can't bring myself to buy one and send it off to him, because where will it all end if I do that? Lego sets for Christmas probably.

The thing is though, it's not Madoc's fault is it, none of the mess his father made is his fault. In the end I walked away from the cards and bought two very large cream doughnuts for me and Si Instead, no chance of setting myself up for a lifetime of birthday induced anguish there.

Friday 11th October

7pm

Decided to go to the newly re-established writing group after Mam's, give them another chance.

The old writing group was quite a social event, with cakes on people's birthdays and secret Santa's etc. Our poetry group can't really be classed as a social thing. We sit there, read our poems, dare the others to criticise, drink terrible coffee and then scurry home, a bit of a savage experience really. Anyway, I know the score, so took one of my old stories to read, it was about a robber and his mate who hold up a post office.

11pm

I hate people! The villain of my piece was called John Thomas, but apparently the old blokes in the group don't see this as a perfectly good Welsh name but prefer the fact that "John Thomas" is slang for penis but nobody explained this to me until the end of the meeting, I read it very badly because every mention of the said low life was accompanied by old-fart sniggers and splutters. I hate old men!

I looked it up...... fuck that Monty Python and old men!

Sunday 13th October

11pm

Dai unexpectedly turned up at Rhiannon's with baby Madoc and Maureen this afternoon, he was a bit shocked to see the huge gathering that Sunday Lunch has become. Rhiannon was worried about me and Delyth, but we were both fine. Maureen obviously didn't want to be there, and kept whispering, "I want to go. Now!" but Dai was enjoying himself, catching up with everyone.

We all sat and watched Dai showing Owen photos of Penzance and inviting him down next year. (Except for Mam and Rhiannon, who had determinedly between them wrestled Madoc from his mother and were cwtching him up and smothering him with kisses, poor baby).

Rhiannon asked me to drive to the shop for a Victoria Sponge and some candles, and then we all had cake and sang "Happy Birthday" to Madoc, who blew out his candles with Mam's help and became a bit startled when we all cheered and clapped. He will have to get used to all this fuss if he is going to be part of our family, is little Madoc.

Maureen just glared at Dai and jingled the car keys annoyingly. He just ignored her until she loudly reminded him that her mother was expecting them for tea. Richard sidled up to me and said "Something is rotten in the state of Denmark!" I agree! As they were leaving, I took hold of Madoc`s little hand and stuck a fiver in it, "Happy Birthday Madoc" I said, not his fault is it, poor little rich boy.

Tuesday 14th October

11pm

Had a lovely day off today! Gareth asked me yesterday if I would like to take a trip up the valley to talk to a prospective client.

"Client?"

"Client, yes, he wants to do a Death Plan, I know it`s a bit far to go but he is a friend of Dad`s. He is a nice old man and it`s good for the business to expand into the valleys."

So we are off to the mountains to meet a man called Gerald Williams and then after he has gone through his death plan we are going to have lunch in the pub on the mountain pass road called "The Top of the World."

Gareth said, "I don`t know how to say this, because in my opinion, you always look lovely but…"

I interrupted him, "Don`t worry I will drag out my best funeral clothes, can I wear my green winter coat though? It`s cold in them there hills!"

Gareth gave a sigh of relief, "Of course you can cariad, Pick you up at 10am!"

The best bit of the trip apart from spending the whole day with Gareth was lunch in the "Pub on Top of the World," it was lush. I could happily live up there in the mountains. All that green stuff and fresh air, I could buy a cottage up there when I win the lottery.

Friday 17th October

11pm

Gareth and Caradoc joined me and Mam for fish and chips, I was a bit worried about this, because Mam can be weird but it was great, we sat in the living room with trays because we are all family now, Mam said, and I told her about the pub on the mountain pass and how it made me feel as if I wanted to live there. She said the mountains were in our genes. I promised to take her up there for lunch one Sunday when the weather was nice.

After Gareth and Caradoc left, I helped Mam to tidy up a bit. She put her arm through mine,

"Did you smell it"

"Smell what?" I asked

"Death!" she whispered.

Sunday 20th October

11pm

We turned Sunday lunch into a surprise birthday party for Delyth, her birthday is Wednesday which as she informs me is Scorpio on the cusp with Libra. She cried when she came in and saw Les and the silver balloons he had brought with him. She cried some more when we all gave her presents and cards and warned her not to open them until the day. I bought her a nice present because she is ok really, it was one of those hippy bags from the new age shop in town, brown with orange and blue elephants. Smells like a wet dog.

Think I might give zodiac bookmarks a go, did a tiny bit of research on star signs, what an interesting subject! Rhiannon, Gareth, and myself are all born under Pisces, according to google, it is the final sign and the sign that has absorbed all the lessons of the past. How cute is that!

21st Monday

11pm

Our annual Halloween pub crawl collecting money for the foodbank is in jeopardy because I am still banned from the Green Man. Popped my head in there the other day to check and as soon as I did, the landlord pointed at me from his favourite barstool and said, "Out! Still banned!" how embarrassing. I told Si and he is really disappointed because the Green Man is last on our list and the regulars are usually a bit drunk by then so are very free with their money, so much so that Si empties the buckets into his rucksack before we get there so that he can prove this theory right. He will have to go in on his own or find another person to do it, he is upset now as well as disappointed.

1am

Found an answer to the Green Man problem, I will dress up as a ghost! Can`t wait to tell Si about my inspired solution, he will be so pleased! Just need to get a ghost costume now.

Saturday 26th October

11pm

It`s busy at the craft fair, people are starting to buy stocking fillers. One of my customers, Maisie has six children, she said the oldest is fifty four and the youngest is forty, Barry, Paul, Sylvia, Janet, Michelle, and Christopher. She has designed a bookmark and wants six copies showing six sad people standing around a headstone which reads MISS YOU MAM and written along the side are the words YOU`LL BE SORRY WHEN I`M GONE. I told her she could write a personal message to each of them on the back of the bookmark, she liked that idea because Sylvia is not so bad but the others are right bastards. All this rang a bell with me, because "You`ll be sorry when I`m gone" are Mam`s favourite words, in fact I have told her that I am putting ARWEN IS NOT SORRY on her tombstone, if I bother to get her one that is! She says it almost every week, usually on a Friday after her fish and chips but if she forgets to say it, she will phone later in the week and insert the words into the conversation, regardless of whether it makes any sense or not. Comforting to know I am not the only adult child who has to put up with this nonsense.

I think the residents of Cerrig-Mor are using my design your own inspirational bookmark idea as a sort of revenge exercise, I blame Olivia, she set a precedent and has obviously started a revenge bookmark trend. That's the trouble with living in a small town, the six degrees of separation is alive and kicking here. Although I shouldn't really complain, because the bookmark business is booming. If anyone needed to test the six degrees theory, they should come here and start off with Mam, who knows everyone according to her!

Wednesday 30th October

2 pm

Been asking around for a white sheet, Si finds this amusing as I am unofficially engaged to a man who must have cupboards full of shrouds, but on principle, I am not asking Gareth. (Anyway, they have all been shrouding dead people). Rhiannon said she is sure there is an actual ghost costume in their loft, so I am off up there after work for a look.

11pm

Found the ghost costume, it's a bit long so we cut in a ragged hem. Also found loads of photos of Dai and Rhiannon and their Mam and Dad. Dai's son Madoc is the image of him, says Rhiannon, I agreed with her, but to be honest, babies all look the same to me, bald and toothless. I asked Rhiannon if there is any news from North Wales, she says no, grandma is still threatening to die imminently, so Mam and Dad Davies not able to come home, this has been going on for over a year now. In my opinion, they have been up there looking after her for so long now, that I think they will just stay there, but I say nothing because Rhiannon really wants them home even though they will move back in with Richard, Owen, and Rhiannon, I couldn't bear to move back in with Mam permanently. Rhiannon's Mam and Dad are different though. They are nice, for a start.

Thursday 31st October

__Halloween pub crawl pubs list__

The Rusty Anchor

Pub on the Beach

Ye Old Oak

The Owain Glyndwr

The Dragon's Breath

The Green Man

7pm

Great not having to wear any Halloween make-up, just need to pop on my ghost sheet and off we go!

1am

Back home after a very successful evening, Gareth who is a bit tipsy says he has never slept with a ghost before, very funny. Shattered!

November

Tomorrow is another day

Intentions

Be nicer

Be more interesting

Be a better daughter

Be a better auntie

Write longer poems

Friday 1st November

11pm

Pub crawl was great, we invited Geoff but he said he was too busy and anyway he would have to find babysitters, shame. So, it was just Richard, Rhiannon, Gareth, Si and his girlfriend Anna and me. I just looked like someone who either hadn't made any effort or who had been invited at the last minute, the others looked great. The ghost costume flattened my hair and because I am so short everyone kept patting me on the head, and saying "Who`s the ghost then?" In answer I would just shake my bucket at them and go "Woo Hoo, Give me some cash!" Anna loved it and now she wants to do a ghost walk next Halloween with a prize for the best costume as well as a bucket collection.

Bit of a critical moment in the Green Man, the landlord came up to me and said "I know it`s you Arwen, (I said nothing) but as it`s for a good cause, I`ll lift your lifetime ban, just for tonight" I shook my bucket at him. "Don`t push it!" he said.

Wednesday 3rd November

11pm

Went to Poetry Group,

The sea mist creeps in

Gloomy, silent, ominous

Spilling dark secrets

They quite like my Haikus now, mainly because there is more time for them to read their own poems, which are usually terrible. I really love this one that Stewart wrote though. He gave me a copy of it because I loved it so much.

You should be safe up there

In the valley

In a little miner's cottage

With your dog

And your allotment

And your dream of catching the biggest pike

Ever to brave the River Rhondda

That`s where you belong,

That`s home for you

That`s where I used to go to find you

At night before falling asleep

To dream our forbidden dreams

But no, it`s all wrong now

Here you are instead

At my shoulder

In my head

Calling my name

Wanting to come home

You should have stayed in the valley

Instead of spreading what was left of yourself

On top of the mountain

In the shade of a Rowan

So that now I have no peace

No solace

I close my eyes and think of you

And there you are

A forlorn mound of bone white dust

Cancelling out the you in the leathers, sitting side saddle on the Motorbike, crash helmet balanced on your thigh, smoking a Woodbine, giving me the eye.

Monday 4ᵗʰ November

11pm

Gareth and I have this lovely routine now. He stays at mine on Monday nights and I stay at his on Saturday and Sunday nights, then we see or talk to each other every other day, it`s lush being in love when you are older!

He is here now, fast asleep, snoring a bit loudly, but I don`t mind at all.

There are two thousand registered food banks in the UK. It`s 2019 for God's sake! People shouldn't have to rely on charity to feed themselves! We collected £240. 61p at the Halloween collection pub crawl for our food bank. Brilliant! £68.22 from the Green Man, so Si`s theory still holds, the drunker they are the more loose change they have. And the more confused they are about the notes, is it £5 or is it £20? I find this a bit dodgy but Si says it`s fair do`s and when he goes out on a blinder he is lucky to come home with his life, let alone pockets full of money.

Tuesday 5th November

Bonfire night!

11pm

Trekked up to the headland to see one of the town council dignitaries light the beacon that signals to the fire officers from Ton Mawr that the festivities can begin. It`s so beautiful, I will never get tired of seeing the fireworks reflected in the sea and of looking out for the ones that are sent up into the sky across the water in Devon, hoping there is someone over there having the same thoughts as me. Always makes me feel as if I am part of an ancient landscape, I think about all the others from the past who have stood here looking across the water, I wish we had a bridge, it would have to be long mind. The longest bridge in the world according to google is the Dan-yan Kunshan Grand Bridge in China which is 164.8 km long. Do-able then, a bridge from Cerrig-mor to Devon would be brilliant.

Sunday 10th November

11pm

Dai popped up in his sports car from Penzance to Rhiannon's, he said it was a flying visit, because on Tuesday he had to go on to his mother and father's in North Wales. He was a bit worried about the reception he was going to get there but it had to be done, and he has been speaking to them every week on the phone since his rise from the dead. We were having a fag together at the bottom of the garden, he said congratulations on your engagement, although officially we are still married, you know. All the things I could have said in reply stayed for once in my head, instead I said "Oh thanks Dai."

Then he put his arm around me and whispered in my ear, "I still love you" I pushed him away "We could make another go of it, I'll ditch Maureen buy a big house in the country, we can move away from here and from the past."

I said, "Get lost Dai, I`m marrying Gareth and I`m staying here in Cerrig-Mor with my family and friends. And! I don't love *you* anymore!"

Delyth appeared at the kitchen door to tell us dinner was ready. Relieved to see her for once, I stood up to go back to the house. Dai called out to her, " Oi! Delyth, I think I've found that cookery book you wanted, on Amazon. "She looked surprised "What book?"

I gave him a mean eyed look and left them to reminisce over favourite recipes, I expect.

Later when he took Owen and Richard for a spin with the roof down, I told Rhiannon and Delyth what he had said to me, Rhiannon was very dubious at what he had said she thinks it was probably mischief making because I was with Gareth. Delyth suddenly seemed very agitated and said she had to go home now as Les was popping round for a quick coffee before his late shift in the Spar. I very kindly offered her a lift, but she said she would like to walk.

Monday 11th November

7pm

Popped up to Mam's this morning because today is Armistice Day and she lights candles for her uncles who died in World War One, she has a little cry even though she never met them, they were her mother's brothers, barely out of their teens. They went to war together and died together. She says I have to remember them in this way even when she is dead, in honour of my ancestors who died for nothing, as it turns out. For once I agree with her. Hate to think of her crying on her own for dead uncles.

2am

Gareth and me are all cwtched up watching "The Vikings" he thinks he is so funny by going on about me fancying Ragnor, when the truth is that he drools every time Ragnor`s wife turns up, when there is a phone call off Delyth to say she has pushed Dai off the headland, questions were flooding into my head, I tell her to wait there. I end the call and we rush up to the headland with Gareth phoning Rhiannon and an ambulance on the way. Delyth is lying flat on the ground reaching over the cliff edge, I fear the worst, but she sees us and shouts, "It`s ok, he is not dead!" Apparently, Dai wanted to meet up with her to talk about things, so she agreed to meet him up at the headland. When she got there, he was sitting on a blanket drinking mulled wine from a thermos flask. She sat beside him. He took her hand in his and said, "Remember we used to do this all the time when we first met." Turns out he is offering to move back in with her, and even marry her, Delyth knows he has already tried this on with me, the scum bag, so she stands up and walks to the edge, desperately trying to batten down her anger and thinking of a suitable reply, she said she felt sad and very very angry and slightly flattered by his offer which made her even more angry. He follows her, gets in front of her to look her in the eyes, saying, "It's you I love, Delyth, it`s always been you." So she gives him a huge shove and he bounces over the edge, luckily landing on a convenient ledge but injuring his back in the process.

By the time the paramedics arrive, we are all shouting down words of encouragement, and Owen is videoing the whole thing on his phone.

Eventually Dai is off to the hospital, the police are taking notes and are threatening to take Delyth into custody, but Gareth being an upstanding member of the community and well known to the officers (in a good way of course) persuades them to let us take her home with us and to have her down at the station at 9 am sharp. Police Constable Jason Morgan, who is a big intimidating bloke, goes right up to Delyth gives her a very hard stare and says "I`ll be seeing you in the morning then" he turns to leave but then turns back and said "Don't think about absconding will you"

I say "It was an accident! He probably slipped!" he gives *me* the hard stare then and says, "You had better hope so!"

We all go back to mine for a bit, Gareth helps Owen to do this really clever thing with his phone and my laptop, so we sit there watching the drama unfold all over again. Rhiannon say "Look at the state of my hair! For God's sake, why didn't any of you say anything!" So then Delyth says "And look at the size of my backside, I'm never wearing those jeans with that puffer jacket ever again!" Owen then does something technical and zooms in on the backside, I start snorting and choking with laughter because my mouth is full of coffee and soon we are all crying laughing and asking Owen to play the video again and again, luckily Gareth joins in so I know he is definitely the man for me and will fit right into my weird extended family perfectly.

Tuesday 12th November

8am

Because I always have Tuesday off, I have been press-ganged into accompanying the ex-mistress who tried to murder my soon to be ex-husband to the cop shop! Tamping! Everyone else is very busy and "To be fair," they said, "You look like you could be her Mental Health Social Worker, and that can only help." Delyth is very clingy on the way to the interview, I have to keep saying, "Get off mun! I'm trying to drive!"

1.30 pm

Just dropped Delyth home, she is really upset, I tried to console her but she is convinced she will go to prison. They didn`t even caution her, just said they will be in touch after they have interviewed Dai.

11pm

Popped into the hospital this evening with Rhiannon, to see Dai, he is fine, mostly cuts and bruises and a deflated ego. Doing his best to chat up all the nurses and be the life and soul of the Acute Medical Ward.

Rhiannon phoned Delyth to tell her he is on the mend and that he is not pressing charges. Called into Gareth`s on the way home and ate left over lasagne and watched a repeat of Catchphrase with Caradoc, he got every question right, obviously.

Friday15th November

11pm

Went to writing group after fish and chips at Mam`s, The prompt was "First love."

My story about "First Love." was obviously autobiographical so they all know now that I was dumped by my first love after 21 years of marriage for an air head with nice hair and an NVQ in cookery. So embarrassing!

I have given up the writing group, it is definitely not for me.

Alison said it's all my fault because I don't edit things properly and by the middle of the story I had changed all the pronouns to "Me" and "I" and by page two I had switched from invented names to my own name and Dai's, who because he is a carpenter, is well known to the aspiring writers/loft converting bungalow owners of Cerrig-Mor.

Sticking to poetry group and haikus from now on. I have no secrets from them, we are all wounded there.

Saturday 16th November

11pm

Si has invited me and Gareth to his "Birthday Bash" in the Rusty Anchor, I said yes, of course, but I'm dreading it, all his friends are nice one to one, but are a nightmare when they all get together and drink is involved. Still having flashbacks from last year! I asked him what he wanted off me for his birthday, he asked what the budget was, I told him it was £20 he said he would think about it. I suggested he have a quick look around the craft fair, he did and came back with a multi-coloured bobble hat with detachable ear flaps and a matching pair of gloves. I popped over to Lynda's table pay for them and discovered he had commissioned a hat exactly like his birthday hat for someone for Christmas, I hope to God it's not me.

Sunday 17th November

11pm

No one would go in to see Dai, so me and Rhiannon had to go again. We took Owen with us and gave him free reign to question Dai about his favourite book, which as everyone know is Haynes's guide to the VW Beetle, the dirtier the better. Of course, this interest in other people's reading preferences is just a ploy used frequently by Owen who listens to the answer for a minute and then spends as much time as possible afterwards giving the listener a detailed account of the battle scenes in his own latest favourite. I did a bit of dreaming about me and Gareth when this was going on, and Rhiannon set about writing her Christmas List. When we left, Dai was snoring gently. "Bless" said Arwen. "Owen always has this effect on people, so soothing."

Monday 18ᵗʰ November

11pm

They let Dai out of the hospital today, his back is not right, so he can`t drive properly. He is staying in Rhiannon and Richard`s spare room, and I know from experience that he will have to listen to Owen going on about his latest obsession which at the moment is the rise and fall of the Ottoman Empire. Maureen is significantly absent during the whole drama.

This morning, the council recycling van man had chucked new stuff for me and Betty Upstairs into the front garden, but when I got back home, they were all neatly lined up ready to use, Betty to thank for that I expect. Love new recycling stuff

Tuesday 19th November

Meet Shirley for coffee

11pm

Royal Mail parcel this morning, the postman was examining the new recycling stuff when I opened the door

> "Hiya" I said, he turned around, big grin on his face, "How do you spell bottom?"
>
> "What?"
>
> "As in Bottom Flat"

Turns out, Betty had taken her large black indelible marker and written

Arwens Flat

(Bottume)

On all my recycling stuff, tamping!

321

Totally wasted at least 1 hour of my day off by meeting Shirley for coffee. She has given up smoking (that won't last), so we sat inside Luigi's coffee shop instead of huddling together on the metal chairs on the seafront, which is what we usually do. It was so hot in there! She might have warned me, there are only so many layers you can take off before you get down to the thermal vest, even though I was boiling and looked like a cooked lobster, she refused to sit outside because she was worried about getting tempted into smoking one of my roll ups.

Shirley has a new significant other. She is now engaged to Posh Andrew and waggled her diamond solitaire at me. Followed it up with a lecture on how if I wasn't so picky I wouldn't be on my own. I reminded her that I was not on my own anymore and was actually engaged to Gareth, this resulted in her going on about it being not serious, because "How can you think of marrying an undertaker for God's sake! Is it because of the big house and how rich he is?" I have become used to this sort of hurtful comment when it comes to me and Gareth, it's annoying but not worth a reply. Shirley is easy to distract and loves talking about herself so I said. "When are you getting married then?"

She glared at me, "I am not divorced from Bastard Colin am I? He`s refusing to give me a divorce until I give him the dog`s ashes, the bastard!"

"Oh right" I said. "Sorry, I forgot about the doggie."

"Anyway" she muttered, rummaging in her bag for mints, "Andrews kids hate me, they think I am after his villa in Spain."

I considered telling her how Delyth made pretend ashes from fag ash, but decided against it because the truth is, you never know how Shirley is going to react. She is a miserable bastard. Sometimes I don`t know why most of my friends are actually still my friends. Even though I have known Shirley since junior school we have nothing in common, she nags me to meet up and then behaves like I`m her boring little sister who tags along. She is always giving me advice about how to be more like her, wear this, do that, dye this, shave that. Bit sick of it really.

I was going to be nice and invite her to our engagement party, but I'll have another think about that.

Wednesday 20th November

8am

Si`s birthday today! I`m buying him an all-day takeaway breakfast from Maggie Stamp`s Café. I`ll order it on the way into work. Birthday binge drinking session in the Rusty Anchor at 6pm sharp. Gareth and I are going but plan to escape about 8pm, Si will be plastered by then and won`t even notice us sneaking out.

2pm

Si loved his card and his all day breakfast. He wore his bobble hat all day, he looks bloody stupid in it! Geoff told him to take it off because he was in work not some hippy festival or at least detach the ear flaps. Si said, "Can`t hear you boss, I think it`s the ear flaps. Lovely and warm they are." Geoff then turned on me saying, "Why did you buy him such a stupid present?" Well I am not Si`s keeper am I?

11pm

We managed to sneak away from the Rusty Anchor about 8pm as planned. Not being funny but that is a terrible pub. I have nothing good to say about it. We watched last week's Question Time on the iPlayer which involved a lot of shouting at the tv from Gareth and me saying the W word a lot.

Friday 29th November

Feed Owen`s cat

11pm

Rhiannon, Richard, Owen, and Dai went off to North Wales to visit Rhiannon`s parents. Back home on Sunday. Gareth was coming to Mum`s with me for fish and chips but phoned me at work this afternoon to say that he has to go down to Southampton because Kathy has fallen into an open grave and is seriously ill in hospital, I offered to go with him but he said no, he will call later. When I told Mam, she went on about how in her day there was none of this nonsense about staying friends with exes and rushing about the country to rescue them. Oh no, once a relationship was over, that was it, anything else is just asking for trouble. She has convinced me, I don't trust Kathy as far as I could throw her.

Just got a text off Gareth. *"Missing you, back soon xxxxx"*

Saturday 30th November

Feed the cat

11pm

Really busy at the craft fair, sold quite a lot of bookmarks. Mentioned to Si that Kathy is in hospital and Gareth is down there to see her, he had the same old fashioned view as my mother! He wanted to know where her live-in toyboy and her family were and said it was not Gareth's job to go rushing off to Southampton at the drop of a hat. I'm a bit worried now.

Gareth phoned about 10pm, he had just left the hospital and said that Kathy might be able to come home on Monday as her injuries weren't as bad as they thought. I said "Oh, I bet her family are worried about her," but he said she has no family left, all dead. I asked how he was getting on with the boyfriend but it turns out that

Harvey has moved out. "I miss you so much," he said, he sounded so tired, I said, I miss you too, have supper and get some sleep Gareth, speak tomorrow.

December

Ever thine, ever mine

Intentions

Be nicer

Be more interesting

Be a better daughter

Be a better auntie

Write longer poems

Sunday 1ˢᵗ December

Feed cat

11pm

As arranged, I took Mam and Albie to the pub for Sunday lunch, I hope I never get so old and critical, was so glad to get home. Waited for Gareth to phone but in the end I phoned him, no pickup so I left a message.

Rhiannon phoned, they are home from North Wales, I told her about Kathy, she said not to worry that everything will be ok. Everyone in North Wales is fine but Grandma is fading fast, Rhiannon is still hoping that Mam and Dad Davies will sell her cottage and come back home next year. Richard agrees with me though and thinks they like it there too much now and have settled. I hope not, Rhiannon misses them loads.

If we were going to Single`s Nite! This evening, I could ask the DJ to play the Pogue's Christmas song. Never mind, Si and I can do what we usually do and play it every day at work from now until Christmas Eve. Lush!

Monday 2nd December

11pm

Gareth is home, he came around this evening, he was not right, coughing like a 40 a day man, he told me he had to bring Kathy back to Wales with him because she can hardly walk and is covered in bruises, she hinted that not all of them were from the fall into the grave, leading Gareth to believe that she and Harvey had had a bad break up, he said he felt sorry for her, I was so concerned about the way he looked that I couldn't bear to question him about her motives. He hadn't phoned because his phone went missing and Kathy`s had broken in the fall. He fell asleep almost at once on the sofa, and then left for home about ten, he wouldn't kiss me goodnight, he said he was coming down with something. I sent him home with half a bottle of whisky, some paracetamol, a lemon, and instructions on how to make a hot toddy.

Tuesday 3rd December

10am

Weird phone call off Kathy, she was using Gareth`s phone! I thought it was lost, what the hell is going on!

She said that now that she was home in Cerrig-Mor for the foreseeable future, that she and Gareth were giving things another go, she said he was too embarrassed to tell me himself and is pretending to be very ill, but she hoped I would give them both some space to sort things out. I don`t know what to do!

10.30am

Text from Gareth's work mobile saying he has a horrible virus and I should stay away from him, he is going to bed with the paracetamol and the whisky. He sent another text a few minutes later, "Please don`t come here Arwen, I would hate it if you caught it too. Love you xxxx." Popped in to see Si and ask advice about Kathy and Gareth. He looked at me, said, go get your car. I`ll stick a note on the desk and tell Geoff I`m going out. I ran home and fetched my car and we drove to Gareth`s. Si said I had nothing to lose by calling on Gareth and getting to the truth of it, and he is right. A woman covered in livid bruises and with her arm in a cast answered the door, Si said, we have come to check on Gareth, where is he? He was smiling but she could tell he was not going to be messed about. She looked around him, saw me and said "And you are?"

"This is his fiancé and best friend and she is very worried about his wellbeing. You must be his ex-wife Kathy, we know all about you! Come on Arwen, bring the chicken soup!" I had to laugh, chicken soup. We pushed past Kathy and headed up to Gareth`s flat and found him in his bedroom, pale and very obviously ill. Si took one look at Gareth from the doorway and said, "I`m going back to work, and if you catch the lurgy off him I don't want you anywhere near me, it`s too close to Christmas!"

I called Gareth`s friend, Doctor Morris (Sam), he popped around within minutes! It's not what you know but who you know isn't it! Sam said "A lot of it about, plenty of fluids and paracetamol, and best to take him back to yours." Sam and I managed to get Gareth into my car, he was very weak. I left a note and my phone number for Lucy and his dad and phoned the staff at the funeral home to tell them where he was. They were shocked because Kathy told them this morning that he had left early for my place and was not to be disturbed.

So here he is, looking much better already, shocked at what Kathy has been saying, all cwtched up on my settee. Lucy phoned, they had been to the dentists, she said they were glad he was staying with me because Kathy has been acting all weird and that she will phone Adrian her boyfriend to come after work and stay over with her and Caradoc.

I messaged Si, *"Love you so much, see you tomorrow, unless I catch the lurgy xx."*

Wednesday 4th December

11pm

Gareth is so much better so took him to poetry group with me because he is thinking of joining. Everybody was very nice to him except Gwyneira, she glared at him muttered *crachach* under her breath just loud enough for us to hear. He is not, just because he is rich and lives in a big house (most of which is taken up by temporarily housing the dead), doesn't mean he is *crachach.*

Gareth thought my poem was really good.

Mermaid

I stand in the space where sea kisses land.

Where the pebbles hiss, with the shushing sand.

I watch as the bubbles pop around my feet

And my cold blue sisters beckon and beseech

"Come in, come back, come in and stay"

Ignoring their cries I turn slowly away

I whisper and weep "Not yet, not today"

Trouble is, he had to leave the room when Ryan, the new member read his very rude poem, "Ode to extramarital sex." Gareth excused himself by pretending to have a massive coughing fit, I found him later by the bins, having a cheeky swig out of his hot toddy flask. He had been crying! Crying laughing that is," how the hell can you keep a straight face Arwen!" He will never be able to join our poetry group unless he can keep all of his laughter buried deep inside of him and cultivate a poker face. Shame.

Before we all went home, we all submitted our three poems so that Stewart can get on and publish them! We are going to call the book, "The poetry of Cerrig-Mor" Lovely.

Gareth has definitely recovered from his illness, still coughing but definitely ok, he said the laughing did him good so tomorrow he is going to deal with Kathy. I offered to go with him, but he said no, better not. I looked a bit sceptical but he reassured me that he has finished being nice to her and she will be taking her broken arm and leaving asap.

Saturday 7th December

7pm

Delyth popped into the craft fair and asked if she could have a template and could I make her some bookmarks, I said yes because even though she has caused me a lot of grief in the past, business is business and to be fair, Gareth is the man for me and I wish we had got together decades ago, he should have asked me out in Geography class, then we could have gone to the same university, got married, had kids. It would have been lush but being together now is lovely and as mam says, you can dream as much as you want about the past, but you can`t change it. So I should thank Delyth really for taking Dai off my hands and offer her a discount.

Because Delyth is now a fully paid up member of Mam`s Baptist Church, she has commissioned twenty bookmarks with a very scary angry looking Baby Jesus in a manger with the words "Be still and know that I am God (Psalm 46:10)" for her friends for Christmas. I hope I don`t get one! Bet I will though. I will try to draw the Baby Jesus without the popping angry eyes but the more I look at him, the more I like him. He reminds me a bit of Madoc.

1am

I've been thinking of Delyth having twenty friends all night!

I texted Rhiannon to ask her how many friends she has and then woke up Gareth and asked him how many friends he has, "Um, about twenty I think" he said sleepily. Rhiannon replied rather quickly for her, "About twenty, why the hell are you texting me at this time of the night?" I am really upset, how come everyone has tens of friends and I only have a couple? Am I a sociopath? I`ll have to google it.

Sunday 8th December

11pm

I have made a list of my friends, putting Mam, Delyth and Dai on the list is fucking stretching it mind! Oh yes, I am not a sociopath thank God!

Friends

Si

Gareth

Rhiannon

Richard

Dianne

Mam

Faye

Owen

Madoc

Debatable friends

Jackie (Chip shop)

Shirley

In an ideal but unlikely future-*Delyth and Dai*

That`s thirteen! Two have until very recently been my arch enemies, two are debatable and one of them is a baby! Rhiannon and Gareth said using my criteria for friendship, they could probably get up to about fifty each, so fucking hilarious. Even Mam has more than me, although to be fair, most of them are actually dead now, so they probably shouldn`t be counted. The only person with *less* friends than me was Uncle Albie, which is not a comforting thought at all.

Gareth went home after lunch so that he could give Kathy a lift to the train station in Ton Mawr.

He told her as they stood waiting for the train, that he would never forget what she had done to him and thank God I didn't believe her lies about him wanting to end our relationship because he is convinced she was hoping he would die of dehydration and neglect, so she could get her hands on his money. Wow. I commented on how kind he was waiting for the train with her under the circumstances, he said he waited to make sure she got on it. She was miraculously clear of the horrible bruises that had covered her face and neck, he thinks it was make-up. He is still really annoyed with her. "Don`t come back here again" he shouted, as the Swansea to Bath left the station.

Thursday 12th December *General election*

5pm

Dai phoned me at work to see if he could pop around to flat later. I said he could then I phoned Gareth to ask if he could be there. They are both coming about 6pm. Popped out to vote.

11pm

I still don't know what Dai popped around for, he was a bit dismayed when he came in and found Gareth in the kitchen making coffee, probably wanted something that he couldn't ask for in front of Gareth, the mind boggles. After numerous stilted attempts at small talk, *(apparently he has a new nickname now and he is so fucking proud of it, "Dai what Disappeared")* and telling us about his inharmonious life with Maureen, he said he had come to see if any of his old tools were still in the shed, as Uncle Albie needed brackets on the wall for his new 50 inch tv. "Wow" said Gareth, "I've always wanted to look in Arwen's shed, mind if I tag along"

I never know if Gareth is being serious or not, so I smirk at him and hand him the keys, "Do the honours," I say.

Dai mooched around in the shed pretending to look for tools, although we all know this is an excuse to be around mine, Gareth is in his element, searching through ancient mouldy boxes and eventually holding up a very old and battered Dandy annual "I had one like this!"

"It`s mine" says Dai scowling.

I take the annual off Gareth and hand it to Dai and say "Bless, give it to Madoc, something for him to treasure Dai!"

After Dai spent some time pretending to look for tools, had given up searching half-heartedly through the clutter in the shed and had gone home, we sit and wonder why he really came around. All our ideas are creepy and all involve me in some way. As Gareth is leaving, I give him an especially hard cwtch "I am so glad you were here."

He cwtches me back "Me too. Arwen, I didn`t really have that annual as a kid, just wanted to wind him up, sorry."

I said, "Oh that`s a shame because when you were in the bathroom, Dai gave it back to me saying that Maureen would rather give Madoc the plague than a filthy old book to read and that you were welcome to it."

"Here it is!" I handed him the book. He took it from me, and said "I'll put it back in the shed shall I? There's a couple of old bikes in there that I like the look of, put the kettle on, I might be a while!"

Friday13th December

11pm

Richard phoned and said we need to have a family meeting this Saturday if that`s ok, I said I`ll be there after the craft fair. He wants me to pick Mam and Albie up as well, he will tell them to be ready, I asked him what's it was about and he said, "It's the Dai problem mainly. Don't overthink things Arwen, just pop along tomorrow. Dai won`t be there."

We have a new Prime Minister – Boris Johnson.

Saturday 14th December

Family meeting

9pm

Family meeting at six o`clock with Mam`s home-made corned beef pie and if we are still hungry, her famous angel cake for afters. Mam loves a good gathering and her corned beef pies are to die for. I eagerly offered to take the minutes. They all said "No!" really loudly, but I did it anyway, took my A4 pad from my bag and set it in front of me on the table, then sat there with my pen poised. Richard was uncharacteristically rude and said well at least she can't hog the conversation if she is writing everything down. "Want to bet on that" said Mam, Rhiannon just waved her hand in my direction and said "Go on take notes if it keeps you happy!" well it does actually! A meeting deserves a written agenda and a minutes taker, for a start it keeps everything on track, I would have elected a chairperson, but they all said that was going too far, so I secretly elected myself.

Family Meeting

The meeting was held in Rhiannon and Richard`s dining room and convened at approximately 6pm.

Present were

Rhiannon

Richard

Uncle Albie

Barbara

Owen (refused to leave the room)

Arwen (Chairperson and minutes secretary)

Apologies

Mam Davies

Dad Davies

AGENDA

Dai`s circumstances

Rhiannon`s fears for the disintegration of our extended family

Any other business

Dai`s Circumstances

Dai has handed most of his money over to Maureen which he thought was a better option than being taken to the cleaners by his ex-lawyer, a man of many talents and who has swapped allegiances from Dai to Maureen because he loves her unconditionally unlike Dai, who seems to be determined to leave Penzance and return to Cerrig-Mor. Maureen has told Dai that she is never coming home to live and has settled with the lawyer and Madoc in a nice big house in St Ives. She is planning a big posh white wedding and has bought a Silver BMW so she can nip home to visit her Mam. Because of all this, Dai wants to be rehabilitated back into the community and our family. He has already spoken to Badger who was more than pleased to have Dai back.

Dai was hoping that I would let him stay in the spare bedroom/study until he found somewhere permanent but was too embarrassed to ask in front of Gareth. Everyone agreed that staying with me was a really bad idea, and so we have to put our heads together to find a solution. Albie said he is not asking Ken to move out, we all agree about that too, Richard said Dai doesn't wasn't to stay with them as it is too mentally draining, apparently he has a problem understanding the complexities of the "Fall of the Ottoman Empire" even though Owen has tried to explain them to him on several occasions. We all looked at Owen who was on his iPhone, thank goodness. Richard had already spoken to Mam and Dad Davies and they said he could stay at their caravan until he found a flat, but that is very damp this time of year. Barbara, (aka Mam) who has so far been very quiet, said if Arwen agreed, Dai could stay in her spare room for a while, she could keep an eye on him and it would be nice to have some company. They all agreed that it was up to Arwen who asked for a bit of time to get her head around it.

Rhiannon's concerns for the family

Rhiannon said that even though it was very hard on Arwen, she wanted all of us to continue as we were, one big family with all our quirks and differing opinions, to that end, she wants Gareth, Dai, and Arwen to be able to come to an understanding, because she loves both Arwen and Dai too much to have to arrange her life so as not to upset any of us. Arwen said it was probably time she actually admitted that she was so happy with Gareth that it wouldn't be a problem for her and that she actually felt sorry for Dai. Rhiannon came around the table and gave Arwen a big cwtch, and everybody agreed Arwen was much happier now than she has ever been, even Albie.

AOB

Arwen agreed that Dai moving in with her mother seemed like a good temporary solution to his housing problem, especially if he did the gardening etc. Owen reminded Arwen that Dai hated gardening, so everyone agreed that gardening was definitely part of the deal, as was putting out the recycling and running Barbara to the "Widows Prayer and a Cuppa" at the Baptist Chapel on Tuesdays.

Meeting ended at 7.15 pm

11pm

Told Gareth about the meeting and the outcomes. He thinks all the solutions are great, because he knows that Rhiannon would suffer if Dai and I couldn't reconcile the past and move on, and to be honest, we are all better off if we can be friends. Cerrig -Mor is too small to keep up the war of attrition.

"What about chips on Friday?" I asked.

"We can pick up fish and chips and your Mam and take her and the chips and have supper at Dad's, he will love that! Lucy can have the night off." Perfect!

Sunday 15ᵗʰ December

10am

I phoned Rhiannon to see how things are, Dai is packing his bags and moving into Mam's as we speak! Phoned Mam, she is really excited to have someone to watch Casualty with.

I said, "I bet Dai is really looking forward to that Mam." There was a bit of a long pause, and then she said

"Are you being mean again?" I think I am getting quite nice lately because I crossed my fingers behind my back before I replied, and said, "No Mam! I used to love it when we watched Casualty, and especially when you brought out the special-cake tin and the chocolate liquors." Phew, that could have been stressful!

11pm

To cement our commitment to a reformed reconstructed 21st century family, we had a lovely Sunday Lunch at Rhiannon's with all of us there, she said no board games afterwards as they are no fun anymore, because Owen and I are so fucking competitive. Once again, she has resorted to the F word to get her point across, so I don't argue. Everyone got on really well, especially Delyth and Dai! I was going to bring Les into the conversation but Gareth said, to stay out of it, I did mention afterwards to Delyth that she and Dai were getting on well, she agreed and asked if Rhiannon would mind if Les came for Sunday lunch occasionally, I said best to ask her. So from now on, Sunday Lunch has evolved into this!

Rhiannon's every week

Rhiannon

Richard

Owen

Dai

Mam

Albie

Ken (if he feels up to it)

Every other week

Gareth and Arwen

Les and Delyth

Dai made a joke, we think it was a joke, that he would have to get himself a new girlfriend as he was feeling a bit like a gooseberry. If it was a joke, nobody laughed, after a couple of seconds of silence and stern looks, he added "Right, I'm off to have a fag in the garden."

Friday 20th December

11pm

Cardiff became a city in 1955! So we went to Cardiff to celebrate city day, Gareth, and I both took the day off, Si thought that was funny, "So Friday is a nobody dies day then!" I was going to point out to him that although it is a family business, Gareth is not the only undertaker at Caradoc Jones and Jones, but I can`t be bothered. Geoff agreed I could work Tuesday instead, Christmas Eve that is, I don`t mind even though it is usually my day off because it's lovely working on Christmas eve. Loads of donations for the foodbank come in and the foodbank people get really excited about boxes of toffees etc from the supermarkets, they used mine and Si's pub crawl money to buy soft toys for the kids. Makes us feel all warm and fuzzy.

Cardiff was all bright and sparkly, we arrived about 10.30 and hit the bookshops after a cappuccino and a bacon sandwich from the cafe in the market square. Gareth had brought his rucksack so I didn't have to carry the books around myself.

Scoured Cardiff for two nice rings, both decided that two *"Matching white gold bands, perfect for the happy couple, inscribed with your names and a quote (Maximum 6 words)"* from a little jeweller in one of the arcades was just the thing. I am so happy! We wanted a Beethoven quote from his Immortal Beloved letter, "Ever Thine. Ever Mine." On the way home, we decided that instead of having an engagement party, we would just never mention it again and quietly wear our rings to see if anyone noticed, then next year we will run away for a week and get married in a registrar's office. Thank God for that!

Monday 23rd December

11pm

I know me and Si were starving this afternoon, but today will always live in my memory as the day we stole the egg mayo sandwich platter from the Bingo's Christmas party do, ate nearly all of them between us, hid the empty platter under our desk and then lied to June Bingo Jones about the whereabouts of Doris's famously delicious contribution to the festivities. It was Doris's fault, she rushed in and plonked this huge platter on the desk, said "For the Bingo Party" and then rushed out! We only took a triangle each to begin with, but by the time we had finished there were only about ten triangles left, at first we transferred them to a smaller plate but that looked wrong, who in their right mind makes just ten triangles for a party, so we ate four more then took the rest to Geoff's office with a little note that said "Enjoy!" This just goes to show that it's not just the now notorious Dylan ap-Ithyl who can appear to be good on the surface but is evil inside, it applies to me and Si as well, because when someone from Bingo was sent down to pick up the egg mayo platter we lied to her face and swore we hadn't seen it. Karma kicked in about 4pm, with us both suffering from gas problems, thankfully it was also time to go home. Si said, "I will never eat another egg mayo sandwich ever again." Well that`s a lie as well!

I don`t understand why Si and me can`t be trusted with food not meant for our personal consumption?

Tuesday 24th December

Christmas Eve

11pm

Christmas Eve! Popped up to Rhiannon`s mulled wine and nibbles do, it was really nice. Dai What Disappeared was there with his new girlfriend and her two little children, they were very sweet and there was a lot of rummaging in the Birthday Box for suitable presents to give them both. Mam had the best idea, she handed them both a tenner and said "Welcome to the family, boys," which was really sweet, but as I`ve said before, she is great with other people`s kids.

"Don't hang about, do you?" said Les.

Dai winked at him, "Life is too short Les, too short"

Christmas dinner tomorrow will be a huge gathering, luckily it is lunch not dinner, dinner is at Gareth's dad's house later, 7pm sharp said Lucy Weekes.

Wednesday 25th December *Christmas Day*

11pm

We all had a lovely day, ate far too much food, and the adults drank far too much wine. Gareth and I had to walk to his place afterwards, "Good job your sparkly Christmas dress goes with your birthday walking boots," he says, I think he is joking but who can tell, I can't. I have promised to go back to Rhiannon's in the morning to help with the clearing up.

Thursday 26th December *Boxing Day*

11pm

I left Gareth asleep and went to help with the clearing up at Rhiannon's. She, I and Owen had breakfast together in the kitchen before we started on the dining room, "Just like the old days." says Owen, who is sitting between us scoffing toast, which makes us both laugh.

"Why is that?" I asked.

"He means when you and Dai always stayed here for Christmas Arwen," said Rhiannon, so I laughed again and said "Better than the old days Owen! You have a *huge* weird family now and a new baby cousin and possibly two others if Uncle Dai marries his new girlfriend!"

"I know" he said, "Uncle Dai said we will all have mate's rates funerals, thanks to you, which will save us all a heap of money, especially me!" No answer to that really. I'll let Gareth know!

After lunch, Gareth and I went for a stroll on the beach, found a huge tree trunk which would have looked great in my garden. Gareth refused to help me drag it home, so we sat on it instead and threw pebbles at the sea.

31st December *New Year's Eve*

7pm

I thought how the past year was all about improving my life and getting on with it, and my 2019 list definitely showed intent even if it seemed a bit ambitious at the time!

New Year intentions January 2019

Give up smoking.

Go out more.

Find a new hobby.

Be nicer.

Be more interesting.

Do the lottery.

Find a new job.

Get a boyfriend

Be a better daughter.

Be a better auntie.

Find a carer for Albie.

Write longer poems

Find out what happened to Dai.

And here we are, my last journal entry for this year! I`m proud of myself for keeping it up and getting to December 2019 much happier and with a future to look forward to! As for my intentions list, I`m not even sure that most of the ones *I haven't* crossed off are actually things that can ever *be* achieved to be honest. But if so, I'd better get a move on, less than 5 hours until 2020!

New Year intentions not ticked off

Be nicer.

Be more interesting.

Be a better daughter.

Be a better auntie.

Write longer poems

The last evening of the year is going to be so different to New Year's Eve in 2018. Then I still had ridiculous dreams about Dai turning up again, alive and contrite and of us getting back together. This year is going to be all about me and Gareth looking forward to the future, taking some time off to go traveling, I want to go to Ireland! Thinking of how we can move in together, his upstairs loft which has no garden, just neat landscaped grounds for the newly bereaved or my cosy little flat with its bird garden aka messy wild jungle bit and a mad dog and a nosy old woman for neighbours. Roll on 2020!

2am

Technically it`s January the 1st, but we have just got back and are having a quick cup of hot chocolate before we go to bed. This evening, I asked everyone whether I have improved in the following areas:

Be nicer.

Be more interesting.

Be a better daughter.

Be a better auntie.

Write longer poems

They were all too busy enjoying themselves and getting a bit tipsy to answer, except Owen, who said "I don't really know, would you like to play Super Mario All-stars with me while I have a think about it." Turns out I`m still no good at Super Mario which really annoys him but he said he could never get a better Auntie than me! One more to cross off the list then.

Gareth handed me my hot chocolate, sat next to me, took my pen and my journal off me, and did this.

~~Be nicer.~~

~~Be more interesting.~~

~~Be a better daughter.~~

~~Be a better auntie.~~

~~Write longer poems~~

Arwen`s To do list for 2020

Get divorced

Get married

Onwards and upwards as the great man says.

This is Arwen signing off! 2020 is going to be a fantastic year! Can`t wait!

Printed in Dunstable, United Kingdom